LOST IN
GHOSTVILLE

BY JOHN BLADEK

Capstone Young Readers
a capstone imprint

Published by Capstone Young Readers
A Capstone Imprint
1710 Roe Crest Drive
North Mankato, Minnesota 56003
www.mycapstone.com

Text copyright © 2016 John Bladek

Cataloging-in-Publication Data is available on the Library of Congress website.
ISBN: 978-1-62370-776-7 (paper over board)
ISBN: 978-1-4965-3362-3 (eBook PDF)

Summary: Amateur ghost-hunter Trey Newton can't find a single spook, but it's
not because his homemade ecto-meter doesn't work. Someone has kidnapped all
the ghosts in town, including his Grandma! Suddenly, Trey's goofy plan to get on
TV and meet his hero — famous ghost-hunter Rex Rangler — turns into a race to
save his beloved Grandma's spirit.

Designer: Kristi Carlson
Cover Illustrator: Charlie Bowater
Design Element: Shutterstock: Reinhold Leitner

Printed and bound in China.
009515F16

To Mom and Dad, wishing you were here.

CONTENTS

CHAPTER ONE

A GHOST IN THE GIRLS' BATHROOM

I looked around my sixth-grade classroom. Kids sat up straight at their desks and chewed on erasers or picked noses, waiting for our weekly math test. My teacher, Mr. Brakenbush, glanced at the clock and leaned over to scoop up a pile of papers. A tiny beep went off in my pocket. I had to go.

I threw up my hand.

"No, Trey." Mr. Brakenbush rolled his eyes. "You cannot go to the bathroom. We're taking a test."

"But I really have to go . . . right now." I crossed my legs to look like I was holding it in.

Mr. Brakenbush grunted. "Quiet, Trey. You should have gone before."

"I forgot."

He drummed his fingers on his desk and stared up at the ceiling. I squirmed and pulled my hair and puffed my cheeks, wondering how best to look like I was about to burst. When the ecto-meter sounded I only had minutes, if not seconds, before the ectoplasmic signal dissipated and I lost my chance. A pee emergency was always the best way to get out of class.

After half a minute of watching me dance in my chair, Mr. Brakenbush sighed and dropped his left eyebrow, the really bushy one. The one with the bird's nest in it.

My pocket beeped again. Hunching over to cover the sound, I checked Brakenbush's eyebrow for any sign that he'd heard.

"I'll go with him," Hardy said. "Make sure he doesn't dawdle." Hardy's been my best friend since I wandered into his back yard when we were three. He'll take any excuse to get away from a test, even using words like "dawdle."

"Be quiet and keep your eyes on your own test, Hardy." Mr. Brakenbush nodded at me. "Go, Mr. Newton. You have three minutes before your grade drops."

I checked the clock and made for the door. Hardy snagged my sleeve on the way by. "Get me some candy from the machine."

"There's no candy in the machine, just nutritious junk."

"Two minutes, forty-five seconds." Mr. Brakenbush tapped his watch. "Don't make me change my mind."

"Gotta go." I shot out of the room like water from a fire hose.

Once I'd cleared Mr. Brakenbush's pee-stopping gaze, I pulled out my ecto-meter and checked the readings. It was beeping like mad and the screen on my mobile ghost tracker showed a bouncy green line and a series of seven numbers. I had no idea what the numbers were for, probably an error code, but the line peak meant a ghost was nearby.

I have this goal to scientifically prove that ghosts are real. I'd found some really great ghost-finders that the pros use online: the Ghost-O-Cator and the Spector-Detector. But since Dad lost his job he's talked a lot about making sacrifices, and I guess $500 for a super detector was my sacrifice. So I looked up the plans on the Internet and built my own. The only thing I didn't have was an infrared camera to photograph the ghost. But I had my cell phone camera, so no problem.

I peeked around the corner. The hall was clear. The signal had to be coming from behind the next door.

I reached out and grabbed . . .

I froze solid. Staring me down was a great big humongous *GIRLS* sign. Nothing stops a boy faster than the most secret place on earth — the girls' restroom. I checked the signal again. Strong and clear, the biggest I'd ever seen. This was the best chance I'd ever had of finding a ghost. I inched closer. Why did it have to be in the girls' room?

I imagined the doom that would drop from the sky if I got caught in the *Mysterious Chamber*. The rack, thumb screws — anything was possible. I could just say that I was lost, you know, blinded by pee. But Hardy and I had pretty much used every excuse in the book from all the times we'd "accidentally" gotten into trouble, and I don't think Mr. Brankenbush was listening anymore. And, let's face it, teachers kind of expect you to know which bathroom is which when you've been at the same school for six years. On the other hand, it wasn't break time, so maybe no one was in there. I mean, what teacher lets kids out during class?

My cell phone buzzed. I checked the screen but all it said was, *No name.*

"Hello?"

"One and a half minutes left, Mr. Newton. I hope everything is coming out okay."

I thought we weren't supposed to use phones at school. Didn't Mr. Brakenbush know the rules?

"Almost done." I needed more time. "I think they're out of paper towels. Should I go get some?"

"You're wearing pants, use them."

Click. He hung up.

Beep, beep, beeeeeeeep!

The signal was blasting and I was running out of time.

The sign still said *GIRLS*.

According to my favorite TV show host, Rex Rangler, who's totally cool on the science shows *Spirit Trackers* and *Dinosaur Diggin'*, chances like this may come along only once. Rex has found lots of ghosts, but never gotten any video of them because they go into hiding when the cameras turn on. All that equipment scares them away. That's why I made my ecto-meter extra small and easy to hide. It pretty much looked like a cell phone — my dad's ancient cell phone — no touch screen. I planned to find a real ghost then show Rex Rangler himself when my class visited the grand opening of his new Dino Barn right here in town. I could be rich and famous, and then Dad wouldn't have to worry about being out of work anymore. But this might be my only chance.

Ghosts, or GIRLS?

Beep, beep.

Uh-oh. The signal shrank like a leaky balloon. The ghost was fading away. I had to risk it. I crossed my fingers and hoped that the room was clear of the living.

I took a deep breath, then whipped out my cell phone camera and kicked open the girls' room door.

"Get out of here, you freak!" Vicki Winters, all spit and flying hair, splashed a handful of water from the sink at me. "I'm telling!"

Rats. No ghosts, just *GIRLS*.

Unless Vicki Winters was a ghost! I'd thought that she was just a really, really annoying girl. But if she was a ghost that would explain why she'd done so well on tests. When you repeat the sixth grade for a century you pick up a lot of answers.

Vicki screamed again and hit me with a wet paper towel. "Jerk! You're going to get it!"

In a flash two more girls appeared, Glissandra and Allison, both shrieking. "Fig Newton! You creep!" Glissandra's always screaming.

Did Mr. Brakenbush let everyone out of class?

"Get lost!" Vicki took a swipe at my phone. Then all three girls ran down the hall like their hair was on fire.

Beep beep.

The ecto-meter still showed something here. I clicked a couple of quick pictures and headed back to class. Maybe I could still be famous.

CHAPTER TWO

NO PICTURES!

After my ghost expedition to the girls' room I still managed to get a B on my test. It turned out I really did have to pee, so I was a little late. And of course Vicki ratted me out.

Apparently taking pictures in the girls' room gets you detention *and* your phone and ecto-meter taken away, even if you waited to click the pics until everyone had left. How was I supposed to track down the school's spirits without my equipment? And worse, I couldn't show Rex Rangler my valuable data! How was I going to get on TV? The injustice just piled higher and higher.

"Dude," Hardy said during afternoon break while we shot baskets on the playground. "That was so awesome. The girls' can. I can't believe it. That's the coolest. Wish I could have gone."

Too bad Mr. Brankenbush wasn't as much fun as Hardy.

"I had to lick envelopes in Principal Purile's office for

the *Save our Historic District* fundraiser," I said. There is definitely no "fun" in "fundraiser." "And now I can't go on the field trip to the Dino Barn sneak peek."

"That sucks. It's totally Vicki's fault. Why is she such a dweeb?"

"I don't know," I said. "It's not like I saw anything. She was only washing her hands."

"Who am I going to hang with now?" Hardy asked.

His concern for me was overwhelming. I got to hang with Principal Purile.

The Dino Barn was supposed to be the coolest place ever conceived. Not only did the ads say it had *real* dinosaur skeletons and teeth and horns and even petrified poop, but it also had those robot dinosaurs that really moved and ate each other. It sounded totally cool and scientific, but most importantly, Rex Rangler owned it. Our whole class was going on Friday, in two days.

"It's not fair. It's not like I'm the only boy who ever wandered into the girls' room," I said.

"The only one with a camera," Hardy said.

"I waited until the girls left before I took any pictures."

"That was dumb." Hardy said with a loud snort. "Too

bad your mom's not driving. Then they'd have to let you go."

I was nearly blinded by the brilliance of the light bulb going off. I slapped Hardy on the back. "That's it! Great thinking. I will be going to the Dino Barn *and* talking to Rex Rangler."

* * *

"All right class," Mr. Brakenbush said early Friday morning. "Zip it and get in line. Volunteer parents are here to take us to the Dinosaur Barn. Let's show them how well behaved students at Wethermerry Lewis Elementary can be."

Everyone unzipped. "Dino Barn, Dino Barn. It's not the farm, it's Dino Barn!"

"Thank you for reminding me that you watch too much TV," Mr. Brakenbush said.

I smiled and got in line. My plan had worked. Mom had some time to drive in between showing houses for her real estate job. It wasn't perfect. I'd had to do double duty stamp licking and my tongue was still sticking to my lips. I also didn't have my ecto-meter and Hardy was going in a different car. And Vicki, little Miss Perfect-who-gets-people-into-trouble-after-they-innocently-wandered-into-the-girls'-room-on-a-scientific-quest, was riding with me. But at least I was going.

Hardy was excited too. He reached into his pocket and pulled out a lump of something yellowishly gray-green, sort of like barf, but more solid and without chunks. "Know what this is?"

"Your lunch?"

Hardy took a sniff. "Good guess. But I like mayonnaise with my peanut butter. Try again." He waved the gunk in my face. I shrugged.

"It's real live fake dino poop." He grinned so much I thought he *was* going to eat it. "I ordered it online."

"Really? Too bad it only looks like dino poop. Didn't they have any that smelled, too?"

Hardy's smile drooped. "No, I checked."

I glanced over at Vicki. She stood in line, waving her arm at Mr. Brakenbush. She can't resist raising her hand. She probably wanted to tell him all about dinosaur mummies or something else she already bored us with in class. Some people read too much.

Grinning, Hardy handed me a clump of his dino poop. "Here. You can get back at Vicki."

I tried to push it away. "I'm in trouble already." Hardy pushed harder so I finally grabbed the poo.

Just then I heard a car horn. Mom's minivan whipped into the parking lot and screeched to a stop. I shoved the goo into my pocket before Mr. Brakenbush saw.

"Hi, Honeybunch," Mom said, right in front of everyone. Didn't she know people were listening? It was bad enough Glissandra called me Fig Newton. I didn't want to give her any more ammunition. I ducked into the front seat before Mom could say anything else embarrassing.

Mr. Brakenbush knocked on the window. "Here's one more passenger, Mrs. Newton." Vicki frowned and slipped into the back seat as Mr. Brakenbush handed my mom a piece of paper. "These are the directions to the Dino Barn."

"I got the text," Mom said, cutting him off. "You keep those for someone who needs them." Then she rolled up the window and we shot into the street.

I leaned back and thought about how I'd get Rex

Rangler to come check out ghosts with me. Without my ecto-meter data it would be a tough sell. I'd have to convince him that the ghosts in the girls' room were real. I glanced at Vicki. Too bad she wasn't a ghost.

I was glad I was sitting in the front. Vicki sat in the back and gave her know-it-all guided tour of our route.

"And that's the old Crenshaw mansion." She pointed at an ancient house surrounded by an iron fence. It looked like a prison, but with nice shrubs. "Blanding Crenshaw was a railroad tycoon who built his mansion in 1887, made entirely out of railroad ties and . . ."

Mom zoomed by. She liked to drive fast, which was cool. And it cut off Vicki before she could finish, which was cooler.

I ignored Vicki and imagined my conversation with Rex Rangler as best I could, but she kept talking. "They're tearing down all these old buildings from the 1890s to build a new shopping mall. See, some of the houses are already gone. That's why I helped Principal Purile organize the *Save our Historic District* fundraiser at school. We're trying to get them to build the mall somewhere else."

Vicki was behind the envelope licking? She got me into trouble, and then made up my punishment? I took a quick look at the dino poop Hardy gave me. Maybe . . .

Then Mom had to go and encourage her. "But we need that mall, dear. It's being built by that same man who runs the Dino Barn, Rex Rangler. It's a great idea."

Wow, Rex Rangler was doing everything. He was cooler than I thought.

"But he's destroying our town's history," Vicki said. "Look, there's the old library."

I looked out at an old brick building, half knocked down by a wrecking ball. I wished I could have seen it getting smashed. That would have been cool.

"He's just a TV performer," Vicki said. "He doesn't know anything about urban development or conservation, or even dinosaurs probably. He just reads scripts that smarter people write."

She pointed out the window at more crumbling buildings. They pretty much looked like they were going to fall down on their own. Why not give them a little help? And Rex was not *just* a TV performer. He knew everything about dinosaurs, and *ghosts*.

"Those buildings are all architecturally significant," Vicki said. "Without them we'll be just like every other strip-mall-plagued city in the country."

"Those cities have jobs, dear," Mom said. "We can't afford to pass any up."

I knew she was talking about Dad. The bottling plant laid him off almost six months ago and he worried about money all the time. He couldn't drive today because he was looking for a job. He was always looking for a job.

Mom went into lecture mode. "You're too young to understand how important this project is for this town. Mr. Rangler is using his fame to rebuild the city. Why, he even tore down my mother's old house; paid us good money."

I looked out the window. My grandma's house was the one old building I did care about. I used to visit all the time and she'd bake cookies and read me stories in front of the fireplace. Tales of heroes saving the world and funny stories of kids who always messed up.

I liked the ghost stories the best. Grandma always made spooky noises and let me wear old sheets and we'd play hide-and-seek. That's when I first decided to look for ghosts. But Grandma wasn't there anymore. She wasn't anywhere.

After a couple of minutes the car jerked to a halt and Mom said, "Here we are."

Out of my window I saw a row of shrubs and a chain-link fence. "Are you sure?"

"There's nothing here," Vicki said.

"This is the place." Mom shooed me out the door. "The school texted the address: 4321 Antique Ave. It's just around the corner and through the gate. I've got to hurry. I'll pick you kids up at one o'clock sharp. Don't be late." She leaned out the window and blew me a kiss. "Things to do, clients to see. You can give me a report when I come back. Bye Honeybunch."

She hit the gas and sped off, leaving me and Vicki standing on the sidewalk with the name Honeybunch hanging in the air like a nerd balloon.

"I don't see any other kids," Vicki said.

"We're just early." I really wished Hardy would get here soon.

We walked halfway down the block to the end of the fence and through the gate. Vicki stopped and gasped, staring wide-eyed at an old two-story building with peeling paint squatting in the middle of an empty parking lot. The awning over the entrance sagged and tumbleweeds rolled by. "Oh no. This is the wrong place," she said.

The parking lot was completely deserted and I didn't see any lights. Then I spotted a faded sign over the entrance.

"Look, it says *Museum*. And this is 4321 Antique Ave. This has to be it." I pulled out my ticket.

"Do you see anyone?" she asked.

"They'll show. We can wait inside."

Vicki crossed her arms and kicked the ground, frowning. "Mr. Brakenbush better get here. And if you touch me with Hardy's goop, I'll break your arm, Honeybunch."

CHAPTER THREE

THIS WAY TO
THE EGRESS

Vicki and I walked up to the museum and looked around, waiting for the rest of my class to show. I peered through the glass of the ticket window. Everything was dark and covered with dust, a great place for a ghost. Rex Rangler probably set it up that way. He's a genius.

"This is awful," Vicki said. "What are we doing here? This isn't the Dino Barn."

I brushed the cobwebs off the front door and spotted a light and some movement. "The sign says *Museum*. And the Dino Barn is a sort of museum. I think I see someone. Besides, this place is old, just like all those other old buildings you've got people licking envelopes for."

Vicki crossed her arms and glared at me. "Just because I want to save the historic district doesn't mean we're not lost."

Her logic escaped me. "I'm going inside to talk to Rex Rangler about ghosts." I pushed open the door and walked in.

The inside of the Dino Barn looked as deserted as the outside. Vicki dragged her feet but followed me into a big entryway bathed in the light of a sign flashing neon red.

WELCOME: THIS WAY TO THE EGRESS

"Egress? Cool," I said. "See, this is the right place. I bet that's one of the new dinosaur robot exhibits. I hope it's something with big teeth and claws."

"Egress means exit." Vicki had a grammar-teacher fun-ruining voice.

"That doesn't make any sense. You sure it's not another word for 'robot'?"

"They want you to leave as soon as you come so you have to pay to get back in again," she said. "It's an old trick. P.T. Barnum used it in his museum in the 1840s."

"You were there?"

"I *read* about it."

That egress story sounded like a pile of unlicked envelopes. I clutched my ticket.

"May I help you?" a voice said behind me.

I nearly peed my pants. Vicki hit the ceiling. Spinning around I saw a tall man with white hair and white eyes and white . . . everything, except his black suit which looked older and dustier than the building. He stared at me while holding out his hand.

"Oh, you must be the ticket taker," I said after I started breathing again.

I handed him my ticket. "I already paid. We're from the sixth-grade class at Wethermerry Lewis Elementary on a field trip and I'd like to talk to Rex Rangler."

The man kept his hand out but didn't take my ticket, so I flipped it at him. It fell straight to the floor.

"Oops, I'll get it." I picked up the ticket then reached out to drop it in his hand.

The guy just kind of stared at me. I'd never seen anyone so pale, or dusty. His hair had cobwebs.

"Are you here for the matinee?" He was so thin his mouth was wider than his head and his teeth stuck out beyond his cheeks when he talked. "You're early. The film doesn't start for another hour." He glared down at me like he knew I always snuck candy into the theater.

I glanced at Vicki. She was as pale as the ticket guy. I guessed he really scared her. I'd have to tell Hardy, but would skip the part where I almost peed my pants.

"There's a movie?" I asked. "Cool. I guess we'll just check out the dinosaurs until then."

"Refreshments are at the concession stand." He pointed off toward an empty counter. Then he turned and walked off into the dark.

That was creepy. That dude looked as old as the dinosaurs. I wondered where they were.

Vicki stood still and stared in the direction the ticket guy had vanished. "I think I've seen him before. He used to own the old theater, the one they're tearing down. My mom and dad took me to see old movies there before . . .." She stopped and looked away.

"Wow, that sounds like fun," I said, rolling my eyes. Actually it did. We hadn't gone to the movies since Dad lost his job. It cost too much. Grandma used to come with us and sit next to me. Sometimes, when I was little, she'd hold my hand during the scary parts. She said I made her feel brave, but I felt better, too.

"Old movies? Did they sell old popcorn, too?"

Vicki glared at me. "Stuff doesn't have to be new to be fun."

I had to disagree.

"If he owned a theater you'd think he'd be better at taking tickets." I noticed that Vicki still held hers.

"Maybe," Vicki said. "But there was something else about him I can't remember."

"Really? That's a first. Wasn't he old enough?"

Vicki curled her lip. "Why are you against old things?"

"I'm not, not all old things anyway. I like ghosts, and they're old. But I can't look for them because you got my ecto-meter taken away."

"Is that what you were using to spy on me in the girls' room?" she asked. "An ecto-meter?"

"No! It's for finding ghosts. And I wasn't spying."

"Could've fooled me," she said. "Is that why everyone thinks you're a dork?"

"Not as big a dork as you."

Vicki's eyes flared and she punched me in the shoulder, about twice as hard as Hardy ever had. I tried not to squeal, but I think I let out a little "eek" anyway. Vicki took off in the same direction as the ticket taker, leaving me behind. She screamed over her shoulder, "I am not a dork! And it's too bad you don't have your ecto-meter. Because you just saw a ghost."

I froze and stopped rubbing my wound.

Ghost?

But Vicki was gone. She'd disappeared into the dark.

CHAPTER FOUR

GHOST?

Vicki ran off just because I'd called her a dork. If Hardy and I ran away every time we called each other a name, we'd have never met.

And what did she mean I'd seen a ghost? That ticket taker was weird and lousy at his job — I noticed my ticket lying on the ground — but he wasn't a ghost. Ghosts aren't people anymore. According to *Spirit Trackers,* they're an ecto-magnetic paranormal phenomena that mimic the people they used to be, sort of a person echo. Vicki didn't know what she was talking about. If she wanted to run off she'd have to find her own way back.

I still didn't see anyone else. Where was Mr. Brakenbush? I thought this was the right place now that someone had taken my ticket. But where was my class?

"'Scuse me, son," a voice said from down the dark hallway. "I can see you're busy contemplating terrifically important things, but do you think you could give a tired old prospector a hand?"

I peered down the black passage. It looked empty. "Who's there?"

A bearded man wearing a fringed leather outfit and a furry hat appeared out of the blackness. He stuck his hand out for me to shake. "Name's Wethermerry Lewis."

"That's weird. My school's got that same name."

"Really? Imagine that." His eyes twinkled.

"What kind of help did you need?"

"Much obliged," he said, smiling. "You're a kind fellow and I'm in your debt. Been waiting for you to come and help me out." He slipped off his hat and wiped his forehead with his arm. I couldn't tell which was greasier. "Wasn't sure you'd make it."

"Um, yeah." I glanced over his shoulder, looking for Vicki.

"Your friend went that way." He jerked his thumb down the hall. "Seemed to be in a hurry."

"She's not really my friend."

He grinned at me, scratching his beard. "I was wondering if you could help me get out of this place."

"Don't you work here at the Dino Barn?" I figured employees should know about the egress.

"Work here? Oh no, no, no. Haven't worked in years. Sort of a freelancer you might say. And this isn't any Dino Barn, whatever that is."

"It's not?" Oh no. Vicki was right. We really were in the wrong place. "What is it?"

The man pulled out a pipe and tapped it against his palm. "Don't rightly know. I'm a bit lost myself."

"Oh, well the egress is back that way."

"The egress, eh," he said with a grin. "Aren't you a fancy talker? Must be a good school that has my name."

Vicki might be on to something. Talking with big words made me feel kind of smart. But maybe that was her problem. Her words made her feel smart even when she wasn't.

"Point the way and I'll follow." He bowed and waited.

"She hasn't come back yet," I said. "I kind of need her so we can get to the Dino Barn."

"Don't worry. Can't get lost in here."

Can't get lost? Then why did he just say he was lost? This guy was starting to creep me out. Everyone here was weird. I walked back toward the big neon sign and pointed to the doors. "That's the way out."

Wethermerry scratched his chin and stared at the doors, not moving. I turned to go back and look for Vicki. "Bye."

"I wonder if you could do an old man one more small favor?" He tilted his head with one eye shut as he squinted at the door. "These old hands just don't work like they used to. Might you open the door for me?"

"Sure." I felt like I was in scouts again. I hadn't gone since Hardy and I had accidentally burned down our tent with a flaming marshmallow bomb last summer. Maybe this was worth a merit badge.

As the man reached the doorway his eyes went wide and a screeching, sucking sound blasted my ears. He grabbed at me, but before he could take my hand, his whole body stretched out thin, like wet spaghetti, and began to swirl. He cried out as he was pulled like taffy, vacuumed back inside the building. In a second he was gone.

I stood there in the doorway, staring back inside. My heart pounded like ten thousand drums.

Vicki walked up behind me. She was already outside. I jumped a foot in the air when she grabbed the door.

"You don't have to hold the door. I'm not going back in."

"It's not for you. It's for . . ."

"What's wrong? You look like you saw another ghost," Vicki said, her eyes wide.

"I think I did."

CHAPTER FIVE

GHOST HUNT

I knew I didn't have any real scientific proof that Wethermerry was a ghost, and ectoplasm wasn't supposed to talk, but the whole spaghetti thing was weird enough to make me wonder. You don't see someone stretched into a noodle every day. I took a deep breath and shook off the clenching in my stomach, telling myself that ghosts were just an ectoplasmic recording and nothing to be scared of. After I calmed down I realized that going to the wrong place was turning out better than I thought. If there was a real ghost, maybe I could still get on TV.

"What did you see?" Vicki asked.

"I saw a weird-looking old guy get sucked up like spaghetti. Then he just vanished into thin air."

"Wow. Then there are two ghosts."

"Just one," I said. "The ticket taker isn't a ghost."

"How do you know yours was a ghost and the ticket taker wasn't?" Vicki asked with a frown. "I think you just don't want to admit that I found a ghost first."

"You wouldn't understand. Ghosts are complicated."

"So?"

"So I'm an expert, and you're not."

Vicki glared at me and tried to blow a bubble with her gum. She pursed her lips and puffed her cheeks, firing a big wad of spit-covered pink out of her mouth. The blob cracked me right between the eyes.

"Sorry. I'm not very good at bubbles."

"No, really?" I said, wiping off her spit. I thought again about the dino poop in my pocket.

Vicki unwrapped another piece of gum and popped it into her mouth. "If you're the expert, have you ever seen a ghost before?" She smacked her new chew.

"No." I admitted that too fast. "I mean, not in person anyway. But I know all about them. My grandma taught me that spooky ghost stories are just for fun. Real ghosts are a natural phenomenon, leftover signals trapped in rocks and stuff."

"Rocks?" Vicki asked, her face screwed up like she didn't believe me.

"Yup. In the ground. The signals, ectoplasm and things, leak out and that's a ghost."

"Um," Vicki said. "Then I guess it's too bad you got your ecto-meter taken away, we could have used it."

I scowled. "You mean too bad *you* got it taken away."

"You were the one taking pictures in the girls' bathroom. And I didn't tell Mr. Brakenbush. It was Glissandra."

Glissandra? I should have guessed it was her. She'd been telling on me and Hardy since first grade and the "peanut butter and spider" incident. Hardy peanut buttered a dozen spiders we'd captured in the yard and put them in Glissandra's pencil holder. She screamed for a month. Hardy had gotten me into a lot of trouble, but he didn't spit on me — very much. But if Vicki didn't tell on me and she really was interested in ghosts, maybe she wasn't all bad.

"I still don't have my ecto-meter," I said.

"That's okay," Vicki said. "Those ghost detectors don't work eighty-seven percent of the time, and the other thirteen percent they're wrong."

Huh? Eighty-seven and thirteen was almost . . .

"That's not true. This is science. I've seen it on TV. How do you know anyway?"

"Just 'cause." Vicki shifted her eyes back and forth. "Do you think ghosts would hurt people?"

"No," I said. "They can't. They aren't solid, just ectoplasm."

"You keep saying 'ectoplasm,'" Vicki said. "Do you even know what it is?"

"Sure," I told her. "It's ghost stuff."

Vicki rolled her eyes. Like she knew better than *Spirit Trackers*. She bit her lip. "Umm, do you think people come back as ghosts, you know, like to visit the people they left behind?"

I shook my head. "No, I told you. Ghosts are paranormal phenomena, not people anymore. They might look like people, but they're really just a kind of a leftover reflection."

"Are you sure?"

"Yup. Rex Rangler said so on TV. Now I want to find that ghost. You can wait here if you like."

I started to walk away when Vicki rushed up and grabbed my arm. "That's okay. I'll help. I don't want to wait alone."

"Scared?" Her fingers were leaving claw marks.

"No. Are you?" she asked.

"Nope." This was what I'd always wanted.

"Good, then let's look for ghosts," she said.

I pried my arm out of Vicki's vise grip and looked around, but I wasn't sure what I was searching for. The main lobby was lit by the neon sign, but down the hall everything was dark. Then I saw it. A series of impressions in the dust trailed around in a circle in the middle of the floor.

"Look, footprints. The ticket taker can't be a ghost if he left footprints."

Vicki walked over and put her foot into one of the prints. "These are our prints. And there are only two sets. And it proves that the ticket-taker is a ghost, unless he can fly."

I put my foot in a print. I'd have noticed that if it hadn't been so dark.

"It also proves that we're in the wrong place," Vicki said. "If this was the Dino Barn they'd dust the floors once in a while."

Not only was Vicki a know-it-all, but a clean-freak know-it-all.

"I already knew that."

"What?"

"The ghost told me this wasn't the Dino Barn," I said. "See? You don't know everything."

"If ghosts are just reflections leaking out of rocks, then how did one talk to you?" she asked.

"They're sound recordings too," I said. "Everyone knows that." I turned and walked down the hall while Vicki sneered. Did she have to question everything I said?

Empty glass cases lined the walls. I wondered what kind of museum this had been. There were no exhibits left, just the display covers. I passed a hundred-year-old hot dog sitting under a broken heat lamp. Maybe it was a fast-food museum. "Hey, look. It's the ghost of a wiener."

Vicki giggled. "It sort of looks like the ticket taker, only not as skinny."

"Ha. Good one." She was sort of funny, and not just funny looking. "And with a much smaller nose."

We both laughed. Leaving the haunted hotdog, I peeked into a couple of doors. All I found was a broom closet and a bathroom — another girls' room. "Don't tell on me," I said. "I'm going in." I pushed open the door. It was too dark to see and after a couple of steps I banged into the sink. Something skittered up my arm and over my shoulder. "What was that?" I ran back out into the hall, shaking my arm and brushing wildly at my back. "Get it off!"

Vicki cringed. "Hold still."

"Get it off!"

She hesitated, then finally let out a shriek and as her eyes closed she swiped at my shoulder. "Oh gross!" she said. A spider the size of my fist jumped off and raced past my feet. Ghosts might not be scary, but spiders are killers.

"Thanks," I said, imagining being eaten alive by an eight-legged hairball. "You're right. I shouldn't be going into the girls' room anymore."

Vicki smiled. "I didn't really mind the bathroom thing. It was kind of funny."

"I didn't get in that much trouble," I said. "And I got to see inside the girls' room and live."

"It's just a toilet," she said. "I don't think they're so cool."

"That's because you're a girl."

Vicki rolled her eyes again and glanced at an old clock without any hands. "Maybe we should go find the real Dino Barn. Mr. Brakenbush is probably wondering where we are. We could come back later and look for ghosts."

I didn't want to pass up another chance at a ghost. "Let's look for five more minutes. Then we can leave."

"Okay." Vicki sighed. "What were we doing before? We must have done something to bring that ghost out."

I tried to think. "Nothing, just standing around looking lost. I had my ticket . . ."

"May I help you?" a familiar voice said from behind me. Spinning around I saw that same pale guy in the dusty black suit, thin as a pencil with a beak nose. He was still waiting for our tickets.

Although I knew he was just a kind of recording, I was still creeped out.

Vicki stared wide-eyed at him for a moment, then raised her hand. We weren't even in school and she still raised her hand. "Are you Mr. Greensocks, the owner of the Bijou Theater?"

He arched his eyebrows and pursed his lips at her, like Mr. Brakenbush does after six hours of hand-raising.

She cringed and took a step back.

"Of course I am, child. The matinee is in an hour. No chewing gum in the theater."

I snorted. Vicki finally got into trouble for something. Then he looked back at me. "Come this way. We've been waiting." He turned and walked toward a dark stairway at the end of the hall.

"Who's been waiting?" Vicki called after him. He didn't answer.

Vicki grabbed my arm. "Now I remember. Mr. Greensocks was that theater owner. He always made me spit out my gum. He died last year."

I glanced down at the floor. No prints.

CHAPTER SIX

WETHERMERRY

Vicki and I walked up the steps of the museum, following the ghost of the ticket-taker. Dust from the floor as thick as on the pale man drifted up my nose.

"Achooooo!" I sneezed right on Vicki's shoulder.

"You are so grooooosssss!"

"At least I didn't spit gum on you."

Vicki grinned and stuck her tongue out at me. "Now we're even."

"Come this way." The man's voice echoed out of the dark like he was talking through a rolled-up newspaper. I still couldn't see him. "Time is short."

The second floor was way creepier than the first. The only light came from papered-over windows, and spiderwebs hung from everything. I slapped at my ears and brushed my hair as I imagined giant tarantulas crawling inside and laying eggs in my brain. Vicki shivered and muttered, "Disgusting," every few feet.

We inched our way down the hall until we reached a

door hanging on one hinge. I looked back at Vicki. "You think he's in there?"

"It's too dark to see. You go first," she said.

I put one foot through the opening and stepped into nothing. The door was for an elevator shaft!

"AAAAHHHHHHH!"

I threw my arms out and grabbed for the door. I missed but somehow I stopped falling anyway. I felt a tug around my waist. Vicki had a hold of my belt. With a huge grunt she pulled me back from the abyss.

"You almost killed me!" I said.

"What? I saved you!"

"Only *after* you told me to go first."

"Whatever," Vicki said. "I still saved you. That's twice. You owe me."

"You're wasting time." The ticket taker motioned from another door down the hall. "We must hurry. You're needed."

I looked at Vicki. "Needed for what?"

She shook her head. "You go first."

"Har har. Let's go at the same time." Vicki nodded and we inched down the dark hall.

This time I checked the floor with my toe before I slipped through the doorway. Inside sat the guy in the fringed coat and beaver hat — Wethermerry. He didn't look like spaghetti now. He squatted on the floor, clenching a pipe between his teeth. Although he was mostly a pale white, his teeth were still yellow with brown stains. I'd never heard that ghosts needed to brush and floss. He stirred a small campfire. The fire was floating a foot off the ground, and I could see through it to the other side. I wished I had my camera. This was the best ghost sighting ever.

"Howdy," he said. "I see you found your friend?"

"Uh, she's not really my . . ." I stopped and eyed Vicki. She started to frown. "What happened to you? You looked like you got sucked into a vacuum cleaner."

"A what?"

"You know, a vacuum cleaner. They suck up dirt."

Wethermerry scratched his head. "I don't usually think of myself as dirt. Still, no harm." He held up his arms and spun in a circle to show he was still all there. "But it appears I'm trapped."

"Who are you?" Vicki asked.

"Wethermerry Lewis, at your service." He took a slow bow and flourished his cap.

Vicki gasped. "But that's the name of our town's founder. And our school. Wethermerry Lewis died one hundred and sixty-five years ago when he fell off his horse after his horse fell off a train."

"That's right." Wethermerry slapped his knee and chuckled. "Someone remembers. I miss that horse, but ol' Moose always was jealous of the railroads." He grinned at Vicki then pulled his pipe out of his mouth and pointed it at her. "I like you."

"Are you two really ghosts?" I asked. Without my ecto-meter I still couldn't be sure. I needed scientific proof.

"Well of course we are," Wethermerry said. "Proudly dead these many years. There are tons of us dead folk everywhere. Most of the old buildings in town had at least one ghost."

I couldn't believe it. Ghosts everywhere! If it was true, I was going to be famous. But I needed more to get on TV, something I could take and show Rex Rangler. Real scientific evidence.

"Prove it," I said.

Wethermerry lifted off the floor and whooshed by my head. "Isn't this enough to believe?"

"That's pretty good," I said. "But Rex Rangler doesn't let just anybody on TV. I need a video or something to show him. My ecto-meter would have told me if you're a looping visual and sound recording generated by a geo-electromagnetic fingerprint."

Wethermerry squinted at me. "A what? Is that like a vacuum?"

"No," Vicki said, crinkling her nose at me. "He means ectoplasmic rocks."

"Is that what you think I am?" Wethermerry asked.

"Sort of," I said, glaring at Vicki. "That's what real ghosts are."

He paused and looked hard at me, his eyes sad. "You're a tough one to convince. So you don't believe I'm the actual spirit of a man?"

I shook my head. "Nope."

Wethermerry sighed. "You were our last hope."

"What do mean?" I asked.

"We're being hunted."

A cold chill ran through my stomach. "Hunted?"

"That's right," he said with a nod.

"I don't get it. Who's hunting you?" I asked. "Besides us, I mean?"

Wethermerry floated up over my head like a parade balloon, his arms outstretched in superhero-flying mode. Vicki dodged as he zoomed by. He passed right through her left shoulder. I could see her shudder. After one more spin right through the middle of Mr. Greensocks, who gritted his teeth and shook his head, Wethermerry finally stopped his aerial stunts and sat down by his floating fire. He emptied his pipe into mid-air. See-through ashes drifted around the flames, then vanished like they'd never existed.

"I don't know," he said finally. "But they scoured all the haunted places in town and gathered up the ghosts. Men busted into our haunted houses, fancy gizmos *beep-beeping*, and before we even knew what was happening or could warn each other — BAM!" He clapped his hands so hard thunder roared in my ears and Vicki's hair blew back. "All I remember was being pulled and stretched. Next thing I knew I was here, trapped like a rat."

This was getting too cool. "Is that what happened to you at the egress?" Maybe if I could show Rex Rangler the exit that would be enough to get me on TV.

Wethermerry nodded and kicked at his fire, stirring the coals. I saw the flame's reflection in his pale eyes, but the light from it didn't cast a shadow. "Same thing every time I try to leave. Not like the old days at the graveyard. I could come and go as I pleased. Darned frustrating."

I'd never checked the cemetery because ghosts weren't supposed to haunt them. Their ectoplasmic remnants hung around where they died, not where they were buried. I'd have to tell Rex Rangler about my new discovery. I was learning so much science.

I also never went to the cemetery because Grandma was there, and I didn't want to see that.

"You haunted a graveyard?" I asked.

"Sure," Wethermerry said. "That one with my statue at the entrance."

I stared at him.

"The statue that never gets the pigeon poop cleaned off . . . you know, surrounded by the lawn that never gets mowed under the leaves that never get raked."

I shrugged. He sounded like my dad complaining about my yard work.

"I know that cemetery," Vicki said.

"You hang around cemeteries?" I asked her.

"I've been there to pick flowers. And to a different one to visit my . . ." She stopped and looked at her feet. "Never mind. Anyway, cemeteries are important and they're going to pave over that one. I'm sending around a petition." Of course she was.

"Pave over?" Wethermerry shook his head. "Nothing's the same anymore. In my day we had respect for the dead. 'Course in my day I was alive, too, so I didn't much notice."

"Why would anyone kidnap ghosts?" Vicki asked. "I don't get it."

"Right with you, missy," Wethermerry said. "It's a mystery to me, too."

Missing ghosts sounded like a great TV episode. I looked around the room. "Makes sense to me. Then you wouldn't have to go looking for them. You'd have your own ghosts all the time. So, where are all the other ghosts?"

Wethermerry frowned and patted Mr. Greensocks on the shoulder. A cloud of ghost dust flew up and orbited his head. "Just the two of us left. Took the others somewhere, but we hid out and they didn't find us. That's what we need you for — to locate our friends and help set us free so we can go back to haunting, or move on."

"Me? Why me?" I asked.

"I heard tell that you know all about ghosts."

I frowned. Talking ectoplasm was one thing, but . . . "How do you know that?"

"A friend told me," Wethermerry said.

"What friend?"

"Don't you know?" He squinted at me like it was obvious. "She said you used to sit on her lap by the fire and read ghost stories."

My eyes went blurry. I could hardly breathe.

"Grandma?" My voice cracked. "You talked to my grandma? But . . . but she's dead."

"That's right, son. And she needs your help. We all do."

CHAPTER SEVEN

DINO BARN

I stood staring at the two ghosts, shivering at what Wethermerry had just told me about Grandma. Ghost-napped? My stomach lurched like I might be sick. I swallowed hard to keep it in.

I didn't know if I could believe Wethermerry. His story went against everything I'd learned about ghosts. But how could I deny the things that I'd seen? He talked and moved and acted like a real person, except for the floating and passing through solid objects. And how could he know about me and Grandma unless he'd talked to her? And if he'd talked to her, then ghosts really were still people, not just ectoplasm. *Spirit Trackers* was wrong.

I heard a car horn honking outside. The sound of, "Trey, where are you?" floated through the door.

"We have to go," I said to Vicki. "My mom's here."

"You will help us free my friends, won't you?" Wethermerry took off his hat and wrung it between his hands, pleading.

I tried not to shake. "Is my grandma really in trouble? Did you really talk to her?"

Wethermerry crossed his heart. "I swear."

I glanced at Vicki.

"I'll help. You can count on me," she said.

I nodded too. I was convinced. "Yeah, of course. She's my grandma."

★ ★ ★

Mom was waiting in the car with a bunch of new For Sale signs to put up in front of houses around town. Nobody was buying though. "Sorry about the mix up. I was so sure about that text from the school. I don't know how I went to the wrong address. I checked five times. I'm so glad you're okay. Hope you weren't too bored."

Vicki and I looked at each other. "No, we weren't bored," I said. It was a good thing Mom got the address wrong.

I should have been all excited about seeing ghosts, but I kept thinking about Grandma. My stomach did spins and my mouth was dry. I couldn't stop licking my lips.

What was I going to do?

"Here we are," Mom said. We pulled up in front of the real Dino Barn, a huge new exhibition hall down by the river covered with flags and banners. "Right place this time."

I swallowed and opened my mouth to say something to Mom, but no words came out, just a tiny squeak. I didn't know what to say. If I told her about Grandma she might worry too much. She worried all the time anyway about Dad being out of work and about money. And what if she thought I was crazy. That would be even more to worry about.

"Have fun," she said.

"Okay. I will."

* * *

Once we went inside Vicki found our class and we joined the group. Kids ran back and forth screaming about dinosaurs. I leaned against a wall and imagined all kinds of horrible places Grandma might be. All those scary haunted houses or rat-filled dungeons and bottomless pits I read about spun through my head on a wheel of horror. I always counted on Grandma to tell me things would be okay, but this time she was the one in trouble. I didn't know what to do.

"There you are," Hardy said. He raced up and slugged my shoulder. He was wearing a Dino Barn hat and playing with his gooey dino poop. "You're missing out."

Hardy dragged me along and we spent the rest of the morning checking out the dino robots and fossil exhibits. Luckily this sneak peek before the grand opening was a little late getting started so I hadn't missed much. There were dinosaur skeleton displays everywhere and even a rollercoaster on the inside, the Tyrannosaurus Flex, which of course cost too much for me to ride. Hardy had money but didn't seem to care.

"Wow!" Hardy said. "Look, it's real fossil dino poop. I need some of that."

I checked out the source of Hardy's excitement. A chunk of stony stuff the size of a football and shaped like soft ice cream — it even had a little curl on top — sat in a gigantic glass case under a spotlight. Little bugs floated just beneath the surface of the poop, and prehistoric flies were glued to the outside. "That's a really big display for some poop."

"It's really big poop." Hardy's eyes glowed.

"It's called a coprolite." Vicki had decided to hang with me now that we were on a secret mission. "From an apatosaurus. They ate mostly plants. And those flies are fake." She was still an annoying know-it-all.

"You would know," Hardy said. "You're such a big poop yourself." He held up his glob of fake dino doo-doo and shook it at Vicki.

"Hardy!" Mr. Brakenbush yelled from across the room.

Hardy slipped his goop back into his pocket. "This trip is no fun."

Just then, green, red, and blue lights flashed on and off and swirled around the room. Music blared from overhead speakers, drums pounding and horns blowing. A big spotlight pointed a beam at the middle of a stage set up near the triceratops robot and a tall man with wild hair, a mustache the size of my arm, and a blinking suit covered with dinosaurs stepped into the circle of light.

Grabbing a microphone he shouted, "Dino Barn, Dino Barn, it's not the farm, it's Dino Barn! Welcome to the brand new Dino Barn, ladies and gentlemen. I'm Rex Rangler, and I hope you're all enjoying your visit." He clapped his hands into the mic so it echoed through the speakers.

Rex Rangler! Wow, there he was. My biggest hero in person. This should have been cool, but I couldn't forget about Grandma.

Vicki glared at him, probably imagining him tearing down old houses.

My whole class gathered around the stage along with the kids from a couple of other schools who were there too. Everyone except Hardy, who stayed and stared at the poop.

"These fearful monsters of the past," Rangler said, waving his hands at the robots, "are brought to life for your enjoyment and edification." He winked and twirled his mustache at Ms. Warful, the new fifth-grade teacher standing at the front of the crowd. "Marvel at the triceratops and his menacing horns and impervious armor as he fends off all attackers. Thrill to the mighty roar and vicious teeth of Tyrannosaurus rex, king of the dinosaurs and master of the earth 65 million years ago, a dark and distant age before the arrival of man."

As he talked the robots sprang to life, spewing steam and roaring above the noise of the crowd. The triceratops ducked its head and lashed out with its horns at the tyrannosaurus, which dodged the strike and plunged its teeth into the triceratops's neck. Everyone cheered or screamed as a fountain of fake blood shot into the air; everyone, that is, except for Hardy, who was still looking at poop.

"Fun, huh?" Rangler said. "Unless you're that triceratops. But the Dino Barn is just the beginning of Rangler Enterprises' massive new project that will completely remake our fair city of Lewisville. Dino Barn, the new Old-Town Mall, and next up . . ." The drums rolled again and a curtain lifted behind him to show a giant screen displaying a video of an old-looking mansion with a creaky porch and sagging roof. A big, black orb, looking like a witch's cauldron with the lid on, smoked and steamed behind a grimy window. Bats flitted in and out of the picture and a vulture perched on the porch roof. A black cat squatted on the steps. The house sat in a yard of gnarled old trees, surrounded by an iron gate with spikes on top. He was renewing the city with a crumbling mansion? We had tons of those already. Mom was putting For Sale signs up in front of them.

"Next up is Ghostville!" Rangler said. "This haunted house-museum promises to be as big a tourist attraction as the Dino Barn and part of the same gigantic complex. The two will provide a dual look into our past and a vital cog in the economic revival of our fair city. Visitors will see the old buildings from town, carefully recreated here on the site, and be regaled with stories of ghosts, apparitions, and poltergeists; spooks and spirits; phantoms, ghouls, and specters. Tourists will flock from all over the world to see our dinosaurs and ghosts, and together they will be the cultural and entertainment center of the tristate area!"

I grabbed Vicki's arm as she spun to look at me.

"Did you hear that?" I asked. "Ghostville. He's tearing down old buildings to make a haunted house."

"I knew my Historic District petition was a good idea," Vicki said.

"Not that. And it's not a good idea, unless you want to lick your own envelopes."

Vicki glared at me. "My dad taught me about history and those old buildings. They're our link with this town's past . . ."

"I'm talking about Ghostville." I cut off her broken record. "Rex Rangler. Ghosts. Don't you get it? He can help us. He knows all about ghosts. He's even building a gigantic haunted house. Who better to help us rescue my grandma and find the ghostnapper? It's perfect. Why didn't I think of it before?"

Vicki frowned. "I'm not sure. There's something funny about all this."

"Oh, dude!" Hardy cut in and slapped me on the shoulder. "Look at that guy's suit. That's so awesome. I wonder if I could get one like that. And Ghostville, even more awesome."

"I know," I said. "Rex Rangler is way cooler than I ever thought. A ghost museum right here in town!"

"You should've done it first," Hardy said. "You're the one with the plasmo-blinker."

"Ecto-meter," Vicki said.

Hardy looked at her like she'd just landed from the planet Mars. "Doesn't she have a home?"

"That's what it's called," I said. "An ecto-meter."

"Whatever." Hardy turned back to Rangler's flashing suit.

I punched Hardy in his shoulder and then looked at Rangler. "I need to talk to him about ghosts."

"Let's try." In a flash Vicki's hand was up and she was umming and ohhing like she needed to pee really badly. "Mr. Rangler? Can I ask a question?"

Rangler's mustache drooped as he pulled his head out of the tyrannosaurus' mouth. "Why of course, my dear. Ask away."

Vicki glanced at me out of the corner of her eye. "Do you have real ghosts at Ghostville?"

"What?" I whispered in her ear. "What does that have to do with anything?"

Rangler frowned behind his mustache for a moment, and then flipped up a grin. "Well, that's kind of a trade secret, little lady. That's the fun of coming to Ghostville, finding out for yourself if the ghosts are real. Who here believes in ghosts?" he asked the crowd. A cheer went up from most of the kids. "Then come on by Ghostville. Tell your friends, tell your neighbors, tell your neighbor's friends, and learn if ghosts are real."

Vicki shook her head. "I don't think he really knows anything about ghosts. He just turned my question into an advertisement. He can't help us."

"You just asked the wrong question." I raised my hand, too. "Mr. Rangler, Mr. Rangler. I have a question."

Rangler stared hard at me for a moment, then winked and turned on the flashing lights on his suit. They ran in both directions now, circling the dinos and meeting up in the middle.

"Come by Ghostville and learn the secrets of the afterworld firsthand." He smiled, but at the same time he jerked his head. A couple of guys in sunglasses standing by the edge of the stage nodded. They made their way through the crowd right at us.

"What's the problem?" Vicki asked a guard towering over her. "Did we do something wrong?"

The man with the dark glasses stared over her head. "You ask a lot of questions."

"We're in school. We're supposed to ask questions."

"Don't get wise with me," he said. "I think it's time for you to go."

Vicki backed off. I didn't get the hint. "But I need to talk to Mr. Rangler."

"Mr. Rangler isn't seeing anyone, especially not nosy kids. He's a busy man."

"But . . ."

The guard grabbed my sleeve and pulled me over toward Mr. Brakenbush. "Is this boy yours?"

"Trey, what did you and Hardy do now?" Mr. Brakenbush crossed his arms and stared at us.

"Nothing. I just wanted to ask a question."

"He was bothering Mr. Rangler," the guard said. "Please keep your kids under control."

As the guard let go and walked off, Mr. Brakenbush flared his nose at me. "What am I going to do with you, Trey?" He shook his head. "I should have left you at school."

"But . . ."

"No buts. I see many envelopes in your future."

My tongue dried up. How was I going to help Grandma now?

Suddenly Vicki cut in. "It's not like that, Mr. Brakenbush. Trey just wanted to ask about ghosts and the guard got all upset for no reason. It wasn't his fault."

Mr. Brakenbush looked at Vicki, then at me, then back and forth. "All right. Trey, you're off the hook this time. But you better be careful from now on." He shook his finger in my face.

"I will."

"Thanks for saving me from detention," I said to Vicki as Mr. Brakenbush herded the class back out of the building. I wouldn't have to sit in the principal's office, but I'd missed my chance to ask Rex Rangler to help me find Grandma.

CHAPTER EIGHT

DAD'S NEW JOB

After school I rode my bike home and sat in my bedroom staring at my ecto-meter. It was Friday and Mr. Brakenbush had given it back at the end of the day. I wondered if that was because of Vicki too. I had to admit that she was becoming kind of helpful.

I closed my eyes and tried to control the hurricane racing through my head. Learning about Grandma's ghost brought back that horrible week two years ago. One day Grandma came down with a terrible headache and she called Mom to take her to the hospital. I wanted to visit but Mom told me Grandma needed her rest. On the third day Mom came from the hospital and I begged her to take me after school. I started to shiver as she hid her tears. Grandma wasn't coming home. I crawled under my bed with my books and didn't come out until the funeral. But I was too scared to go inside the church. I sat outside in the car by myself, pretending Grandma was there to hold my hand. I never said good-bye.

Grandma was always there for me when I needed her. On my very first day of school I rode the bus home, but a huge dog at the bus stop barked at me and Hardy. Hardy ran one way and the dog chased me the other. I hid in someone's garage until the dog left, but I couldn't find my way home. I sat behind a car, shivering and hugging my knees, wondering how long I had before the dog ate me. Then I heard a voice calling for me. Grandma came and gave me a big hug and walked me home. She said she was really scared, but that she felt better because I was so brave.

"I'll find you, Grandma. I promise."

I kept wondering if I should tell Mom and Dad. They were always so preoccupied with money and jobs. They didn't say anything about it while I was around, but at night after I went to bed I could hear them talking. Maybe they thought I didn't know, but it was hard to hide. I'd asked Dad about jobs a few times, but he just told me not to worry.

I decided to give it a try at dinner anyway.

"Um, Mom?" I asked while wiping rice off my face. Ever since Dad had lost his job we ate some kind of rice thing almost every night. Dad and I both had little pieces stuck to our chins. "You know that show I like, *Spirit Trackers*? Well, see, they're opening this new Ghostville place next to the Dino Barn and . . ."

"Not just yet, honey," Mom said. "Your dad has a big announcement. Go ahead, dear."

This was weird. Dad used to tell jokes and be all funny at dinner, but since he lost his job he mostly ate in silence. He brushed off a chunk of rice and cleared his throat. He had a big smile. "Speaking of Ghostville, I heard about it. Sounded really interesting."

"Really?" I said. "Cause I think that the owner . . ."

"Rex Rangler," Dad said. "He's got ideas. Real mover and shaker. Terrific person to be connected with."

"Yeah. That's why I want to talk to . . ."

He cut in again. "As a matter of fact, you're looking at Ghostville's newest employee."

Mom jumped up and hugged Dad across the table. "That's so wonderful. When do you start?"

"Ghostville's opening in the next two weeks. So there's plenty of setup to do. I'll be driving a truck and moving things starting tomorrow."

"It must feel so good." Mom grinned like it was Christmas morning.

"It does," Dad said. "It really does. Now maybe we can afford more than rice every night. What do you think of that, Trey?" He held up his hand for a fist-bump. I tapped his knuckles. "Maybe we'll go out for burgers tomorrow to celebrate. How's that sound?"

"Great." We hadn't gone out in months, not even for ice cream.

"Or maybe pizza. Would you like that better?"

"Burgers, pizza, whatever."

"Great, pizza it is."

"Um, Dad, do you know Rex Rangler? Because I need to ask him . . ."

Dad shook his head. "Can't do that. Mr. Rangler is a very private person, very busy. We were warned not to bother him with any problems. I heard a couple of guys got fired just for talking to him. Plus there are those guards around him all the time. Pretty touchy. I guess that's the way those TV stars live, though. Too big for the little people like us." He grinned. "But as long as I get paid, makes no difference to me."

My heart dropped. Dad had been looking for a job since last year when they closed the bottling plant. Every night he came home from searching for work, flopped into his chair, and stared at the wall. We hardly ever played catch anymore. He was too busy checking the want ads online. Mom tried to show as many houses as possible, but no one was buying. I couldn't get him in trouble at his new job. I was going to have to find Grandma on my own.

Dinner didn't look good anymore, so I pulled out my ecto-meter. I scrolled through all my old readings. It was a pretty short list. Except for the Vicki sighting in the bathroom there was only that same error code, a series of seven numbers. I'd gotten them four times since Mr. Brakenbush took the meter away. I wished I could have tested it on Wethermerry.

Stupid ecto-meter. Why couldn't it just light up and tell me where Grandma was?

"Trey, please don't play with that at the table," Mom said. I tucked the meter back in my pocket as she squinted at me. "What the matter? Not hungry? Sorry we don't have pizza tonight, but I've got rice pudding for dessert."

"I think I'll just go to my room." That was dumb. Mom was sure to know something was wrong. Rice pudding might be made out of rice, but it was still pudding, and I never turned down pudding.

"I've never seen you skip dessert before," she said. "Is there something you want to talk about?"

"No, I'm okay. Just not hungry."

Mom reached over and put her hand on my head. "You're not getting sick are you?"

"No, Mom, I'm fine."

"Let me get the flashlight."

Every time Mom thought I was sick she stuck a light down my throat to look for disease. Grandma used to do the same thing, but she always said she was looking for ghosts in my mouth. Mom went to the kitchen junk drawer and pulled out a flashlight and turned it on. "Open up." She aimed the beam toward my innards.

I stuck out my tongue. "Aaaahhhhhhh."

"I don't see anything." Mom pulled down my right eyelid, looking for ooze or terminal redness. "But you're pale as a ghost. Maybe you should go to bed."

I didn't want to say anything. Everyone was happy

for once, so I just smiled and faked it. "I'm not sick. Seriously. I just have homework." That sounded even more stupid. If I didn't shut up Mom would have me in the hospital next.

I got up and put my plate in the sink then dashed upstairs to my room and closed the door. I dived on my bed and hid under the pillow. I didn't know what else to do.

A couple of minutes later Mom knocked. She opened the door and peeked in. She held an armful of books.

"Can I come in?" she asked. I pulled my head out from under the pillow and nodded. She sat next to me on the bed. "I haven't read to you in a long time, but I remember how much you loved it when Grandma read you stories. These were from her house."

I stared up at the ceiling. "Mom, where do you think she is?"

Mom leaned over and kissed the top of my head. "Well, your grandma is in a better place, a place where she doesn't have anymore worries. A place where she's happy."

"Do you think she remembers us, or misses us?"

"I'm sure she does, honey. She loved you very much. I know I miss her every day."

I glanced at the books. They were mostly little kid books, but one was a collection of ghost stories for older kids. *Spook's Bones* was my favorite. It was the first story I ever read on my own, but Grandma also read it to me a hundred times. "I want that one."

It was about two boys who meet a ghost and dig up, then rebury, his bones so he can find peace and stop haunting the room above their garage. When Grandma first read it to me, I was kind of scared, but later it was just fun. Dad made me fill in all the holes I dug in the yard looking for skeletons.

Mom read a few pages when I started to feel silly. "I'm kind of old to be read to."

"You're never too old," Mom said mussing my hair. "I'll leave the book if you want to read it yourself." She got up, stopping by my desk to blow dust off my model airplanes. "Things are going to be better. Your dad has a new job. You don't have to worry so much."

I wanted to tell her my real worries but my mouth overruled my brain.

"Thanks, Mom."

After she left I called Hardy and told him to meet me the next morning so we could look for ghosts. But Hardy wasn't enough. I needed someone else, too.

I stared at the phone wondering if I should. My hand got all sweaty and my heart raced. Why was this such a big deal? It was just a phone call. Vicki had offered to help, and she already knew the whole ghost story. But I'd never called a girl before. Would it sound weird? What if her mom or dad answered? What was Hardy going to say if I brought someone else along to help, especially someone he didn't like except to tease?

I flipped open *Spook's Bones* again and looked through some of the pictures of the kids talking to the ghost. After ten minutes I took a deep breath and dialed the number.

I was still listening to my heart thump when someone picked up on the first ring. "Hello?"

I was glad it sounded like Vicki and not her mom or

dad. I didn't want to explain who I was and why I was calling. "Vicki?"

"Yes, this is Vicki. Who's calling?"

"Hi, this is uh . . . this is Trey. You know, from school."

"Oh, hi, Trey! Of course I know. I just saw you three hours ago." She sounded giggly. "What's going on?"

"Can you come . . . can you help me find my grandma tomorrow?"

"Of course. I was hoping you'd ask me. I'm totally excited to find your grandma."

Wow. Calling a girl was much easier than I thought it would be. Why was I all sweaty?

"I'll have to ask my mom," Vicki said. "She doesn't like me . . . uh . . ."

"She doesn't like you talking to boys?" I asked.

Vicki giggled again, a little nervously. "No, she doesn't like me talking about ghosts. I'll just tell her we're hanging out. I'm sure it will be okay."

"I didn't tell my mom or dad either. They don't mind if I talk about ghosts, but I don't know what to say . . . you know."

"I get it. My mom doesn't want to be reminded of . . ."

Vicki went silent. Did she hang up on me?

"Vicki? Are you still there?"

"Yeah," she said after a few seconds, her voice catching.

"What happened? Did your mom come in?"

"No," she said. "Nothing. Is, uh, is Hardy coming?"

"Yeah. He always comes."

Vicki went quiet again. I was sure she didn't like Hardy any more than he liked her. "Don't worry, he's okay. Are you still coming?"

"Totally."

It was a good thing I hadn't told Hardy about Vicki coming. He might bring spiders and peanut butter.

"Do you have a plan?" she asked after a few more seconds.

"Sort of. I'll tell you tomorrow."

"Okay, I'll be there." I heard her take a big breath. "Trey, I think it's totally awesome that you're going to rescue your grandma. It's brave. You're really brave."

"Uh, thanks." For some weird reason my heart pounded even harder. "See you tomorrow, about nine o'clock?"

"Nine o'clock. Bye, Trey."

I hung up. I didn't feel brave. I just sat there, wishing Grandma would read *Spook's Bones* to me.

CHAPTER NINE

YES, SHE'S COMING

I was determined to find Grandma's ghostnapper and rescue her, but I needed help. Rex Rangler's help. It wasn't a genius plan, but it was all I had. Hardy, Vicki, and I would go back to the Dino Barn and try to see him again. I just had to make sure he didn't know who I was or that Dad worked for him.

I didn't want to lie, so I told my parents that we were looking for ghosts, just not which one.

"Ghosts?" Dad said, shaking his head as he downed the last of the milk right out of the carton. I guessed I'd have to eat dry Rice Poofies. "We need to find you a better hobby. You know ghosts aren't real, don't you?"

"But you're working at Ghostville," I said.

"It's just a job. They don't really have ghosts there."

"Well, there's a $10,000 prize on *Spirit Trackers* for finding a ghost."

"I guess it can't hurt," he said with a wink. "And it's pretty harmless."

Dad was always convinced by prizes — prizes with money.

"Can't get into trouble looking for ghosts." Dad brushed at a spot that had dribbled from the carton onto his jacket. "Don't tell your mom," he said, grinning. "She'll want me to wash it." He squeezed my shoulder and headed out the door. That's the kind of job I want — one where you can go to work with milk on your clothes.

I waited outside on my bike. Hardy showed up first, choking down a bag of fried pork rinds. I never saw him carrying any food, but he always magically made something salty or sugary appear out of nowhere. He was a junk food wizard.

Vicki rode up a minute later on her purple bike with red and yellow flames, wearing a helmet and a *Spelling Bee Championship* backpack. I remembered that contest. I misspelled *obtuse*. I still don't know what it means.

"I brought a lunch." She jiggled her pack and smacked on some bubble gum.

I hoped the mention of food would catch Hardy's ear, but instead he just stared at me, his mouth hanging open. "What's she doing here?" he finally said.

"Vicki's coming," I said.

Hardy just kept on staring. "No way," he said.

Vicki looked away, hiding her face.

"This is our thing," Hardy said. "Just you and me."

"Vicki's coming too. She knows about ghosts." My stomach rolled over and I glanced at Vicki. The more I thought about it, the more I realized that I didn't really know her. She'd only been in my class since September and I think she was new to the school, too. She raised her hand a lot and answered tons of questions and set up mailing campaigns and never got into trouble, but before getting stuck with her yesterday, I hadn't ever talked to her alone. I wondered for a moment why I had asked her to come.

Hardy's face darkened and he squeezed his handle bars. Vicki wobbled back and forth on her bike. "Come on man," I said to Hardy. "What's the problem?"

Hardy gritted his teeth. "What's up with you, dude? Ghosts are our deal, you and me. Hunting ghosts is for guys, and *she's* a *girl*."

"That's stupid," Vicki said, finally speaking. "I'm the one who first recognized the ghosts."

"She's good at finding clues, too," I said, trying to convince myself as much as Hardy. Why couldn't Hardy make this easy?

He kicked the ground and slapped his handle bars. "Don't ask me to hold your hand when you get scared."

"Don't worry," Vicki said. "I'll slug you if you touch me."

* * *

The Dino Barn wasn't very close and it took us nearly half an hour to get there. The parking lot was full for the sneak-peek grand-opening weekend. People streamed in to see the dino robots eat each other and marvel at gigantic piles of fossilized poop. The lines went on forever. We pulled up behind the crowd near the fence to look things over.

"How are we going to find Rangler in all of this?" I asked.

"We'll just have to wait in line," Vicki said. "But I really think we should be looking on our own. From what I heard yesterday, Rex Rangler doesn't know a ghost from a coprolite. He can't help us."

"That's the only idea I have. If Rangler doesn't know, then I'm sunk."

"Dude." A light came on in Hardy's eyes. "I thought we were going to find our own ghosts. These are Rangler's."

Vicki shook her head and put her hands on her hips. "Ghosts aren't anybody's, they belong to themselves. Trey and I are trying to set them free, not capture our own."

"Who asked you?" Hardy looked at me. "What is she talking about?"

I guessed it was time to tell Hardy what was going on.

"She's helping me find my grandma."

"Your grandma's dead," Hardy said.

"I know — it's her ghost that's missing."

"Dude, wait. Your grandma's a ghost? That is so awesome! Where is she?"

"That's why we're here." I told him the story about meeting Wethermerry and how I thought Rangler might know how to find her.

"Man, this is going to be cool. Ghost rescue. I'm totally on it. But I still don't know why we need her."

He jerked his thumb over his shoulder at Vicki.

"We just do. She's helping." I glanced at Vicki, but she was looking at her feet.

Hardy turned to Vicki and pulled on her backpack. "What's for lunch?"

Vicki yanked back her bag and hugged it. "Some sandwiches, chips, apples, and juice boxes. But it's not time to eat yet. We have to find the ghosts first."

"How come?" Hardy asked. "I'm hungry now. Are you saving some for the ghosts? 'Cause they don't eat. I thought you were supposed to be smart."

"Let's just go find Rex Rangler." I pulled out my ecto-meter. It was easier dealing with my equipment than arguing with Hardy.

Beep, beep, beep. Only a thin green line, flat, and straight, and those stupid error codes. It was Rangler or nothing.

"How does that work?" Vicki leaned over on her bike, taking a closer look. Most people weren't interested. Okay, no one was interested, not even Hardy. He thought it was a video game.

"Well," I said, "it's not working right now. But this green line here is supposed to bounce up and down in the presence of ectoplasmic disturbances. No ectoplasm, no ghost. Most ghosts don't just come up and talk to you like Wethermerry."

Vicki frowned. "Especially the kidnapped ones." She poked at the screen. "Does that have an infrared emanation detector like the Specter-Seeker 3000? Sometimes ghosts don't give off detectable levels of ectoplasm, but can still be seen on the infrared level."

Wow! How did she know that?

"You've heard of a Specter-Seeker 3000?"

"Sure," she said. "I think it's the best detector, but it is kind of expensive. Did you say you made your own? That's pretty cool."

"Yeah," I said, "it wasn't that hard. Basically I just put the ectoplasm detector chip I ordered online into the memory card slot of this old cell phone. I got the plans online, too. Now it's supposed to show ghosts instead of phone numbers."

"Cool," Vicki said.

"I didn't know you were into ghosts, not until yesterday anyway. How come you never said?"

Vicki looked down at her feet again and dug her toe

into the sidewalk. "You guys always make fun of me. I know you don't like me."

"That's true," Hardy said, butting in. "*Nobody* likes you. Now are you two going to get married, or can I eat?"

Vicki's face scrunched and she narrowed her eyes. She pulled a sandwich out of her bag and threw it at Hardy's head. It bounced off his ear and into the gutter where he scrambled after it, wiping mud off the plastic bag. Then Vicki tossed her pack over her shoulder and pedaled off.

"Find your own ghosts!"

CHAPTER TEN

ON MY OWN?

I watched Vicki ride away from the Dino Barn parking lot. She was steaming mad at Hardy for teasing her, and I wasn't too happy either. I told myself it would be okay. After all, I only wanted to talk to Rangler about helping me find Grandma. I hoped Hardy wouldn't mess that up too.

"Peanut butter?" Hardy said, stuffing half a sandwich in his mouth all at once. "That's all she brought?" Crumbs sprayed everywhere when he talked. "I need some mayo. Oh, well, at least she's gone." He hiccupped hard enough to cause an earthquake. "Better get something to drink. Want to go to the Chips 'n Sip?"

"No, I told you I have to find my grandma. Didn't you understand? Her ghost has been kidnapped!"

"Chill." Hardy held up his hands, still hiccupping. "I'm going to help. But that line will take forever. I need a bladder-buster." He jumped back on his bike.

"You're leaving?"

"Yeah, I just said."

"What's wrong with you? Geez! I have to help my grandma!"

He rolled his eyes. "Me too, but I'm choking on that barfo sandwich. Want something?"

"No!"

Hardy hit the road and left me alone. I couldn't believe it. It was bad enough Vicki ran away anytime someone called her a name, but Hardy was supposed to be my friend. We did everything together. When Dad stopped me from digging up pretend skeletons we tore up Hardy's lawn instead. We built model airplanes, played video games, basketball, and baseball together. I even broke Hardy's arm playing football three years ago. I hung out with him so much Mom never noticed when he was there for dinner. He did kind of stop coming when we switched to a mostly rice diet, but I still ate at his house a lot.

As Hardy rode away I sat down on the curb, kicking the loose gravel. My head steamed. I wanted to punch something. I couldn't count on anyone. I checked my ecto-meter again. Still a straight green line.

Stupid piece of junk! Didn't anything work?

Then for just a moment I thought the line wavered a tiny bit at one edge. I stared hard and blinked and rubbed my eyes. The line was straight again. I must have imagined it. I'd never find a ghost with this thing.

I thought about Grandma, probably held prisoner in some terrible pit or dungeon by a demon or something. Now that I knew she was still a person and not just some ectoplasm I wondered if she was scared. She was probably all alone without any friends, like me. Rex Rangler was my only hope. I looked up at the people going inside the Dino Barn. It looked like there were a million of them and nobody was giving cuts. I stared back down at my shoes. This was never going to work.

"Where are you Grandma?" I whispered.

A pair of tires skidded to a halt right next to me. "Back already?" I asked Hardy without looking up. "That was fast." I wondered why I didn't get splashed with his drink. He usually hit me with the overflow.

"I saw Hardy leave without you, so I came back. How come you hang around with him? He's kind of mean."

I looked up to see Vicki pulling off her bike helmet

and running her fingers through her hair. I wasn't sure anymore.

"He's my best friend," I said, shrugging.

Vicki nodded. "Yeah. You're lucky to have a best friend."

"Lucky? He left to get a bladder-buster."

Vicki hopped off her bike and stood over me. "Trey?" She took a deep breath. "Can I ask you something?"

"I've known Hardy since we were little," I said. "He's usually not a jerk."

"Not that. When . . . when did your grandma die?"

I jerked my head up. I'd expected her to complain more about Hardy. Now I just felt a rock in my gut. "Two years ago."

"What happened?"

"She had a stroke." I turned away. Even saying the word "stroke" made my eyes wet.

"I'm sorry," Vicki said. "Were you there?"

"I don't want to talk about it."

"That's okay. I understand. I was just wondering, you know, what it was like." As Vicki looked at me her eyes swelled up like balloons and her lips quivered. I didn't know why she was so interested. I didn't know why I was telling her. I'd never really talked about it to anyone before.

"I . . . I wasn't there. I wanted to visit the hospital, but it was too late."

Vicki closed her eyes for a moment. "Oh. Do you miss her a lot?"

I nodded. "Yeah, I guess so. I mean . . . yeah."

"It's hard, isn't it? Losing someone you love so much. Makes you feel kind of lost."

"Sort of. Why do you want to know?"

"It's just . . ." Vicki stopped and stared off into the distance for a minute.

I'd hidden in my room for months after Grandma's funeral, telling myself that she was just an old lady and it didn't matter that she was gone and I didn't need her. But I never believed it. Now I'd do anything to get her back.

Vicki cracked a small smile. "Should we see if we can find Rangler?"

"Yeah." I jumped off the curb. Finally I could do something. My head ached from talking about feelings.

★ ★ ★

I glanced again at the line of people waiting to get in, buying Dino Barn T-shirts, hats, and cotton candy. With Vicki here it didn't look like so many people. But there was another problem. Yesterday had been free, but today — I should have thought of this before. "Do you have any money for a ticket?"

Vicki dug through her backpack and pulled out a handful of change, not even enough for a bladder-buster. "I spent my allowance on petitions."

"Why are you so into those things?"

"My dad taught me to stand up for what I believe in. That's what he always did."

I nodded. I guess that made sense. I searched my pockets too, a dollar fifty, my whole allowance. One thing Hardy usually carried was way more than enough bladder-busting money.

"We'll have to sneak in," I said.

Vicki grinned. "I've never been in trouble before. It sounds like fun."

"We might run into those security guys." This worried me a bit. That one guy had a pretty strong grip.

"Well, it sounds like fun anyway. Let's go."

Her eyes lit up. "Your grandma needs you."

After chaining our bikes against a fence we made our way around the back of the building on the river side. The Dino Barn didn't look that big from the front because it was dug into a small hill, but walking around it I thought it would never end. There was a path lined with trees that curved around the building leading to a back entrance. A trench cut through the path and workers in yellow vests and helmets jumped in and out of the hole. We skirted around the work and I looked for an opening where we wouldn't attract attention. I tried a couple of doors but they were all locked and had security pads.

"You don't know how to break key codes, do you?" I punched in a couple of numbers but only got a sharp *buzzzzzz*.

Vicki shook her head and popped some gum in her mouth, her cheeks bulging. She was as dainty an eater as Hardy. "No, but there's the loading dock." She pointed to a big garage-like opening. "It's open."

A truck stood parked at the edge of the dock and a man in a blue jacket with a *Rangler Enterprises* patch on the back unloaded boxes. He had milk down his front.

Dad said he was starting work today. I grabbed Vicki and pulled her back around the corner of the building behind a shrub. I didn't tell her that I knew the driver.

"Don't let him see us," I said.

"It's only a truck driver. He won't do anything. We're just two kids hanging out at the grand opening."

"No we're not. We're sneaking in, remember?"

Vicki shrugged and we waited for Dad to drive off.

"What did you tell your mom you were doing?" I asked Vicki while we waited.

She shrugged. "Just that I was going to a friend's house. She wanted to know what friend, so I gave her your number. She might call your mom, so you can say we went for a bike ride or something. Your mom knows me anyway."

"Yeah." I hoped I wouldn't have to answer a million questions about hanging with a girl and not Hardy. I had enough to worry about.

As I watched, Dad unloaded one more thing from the truck, a small crate he left sitting on the dock. "Does your dad care if you look for ghosts like your mom does?"

Vicki glanced away. "No. But he's not around."

"I thought he took you to old movies and wrote your petitions?"

Vicki shook her head.

"You know Hardy's dad left too. He moved to Florida when we were eight. For a long time I thought it was my fault because he was so mad when Hardy and I dug up his yard looking for skeletons."

Vicki seemed to have stopped listening to me. Hardy didn't like to talk about his dad either. "I wonder what that crate is," she said, changing the subject after Dad drove off.

"Dinosaur egg?"

Vicki pursed her lips, still chewing. "Too big."

"Giant dino poop?"

"Not heavy enough. That thing only took one person to carry. Petrified poop weighs a lot. It's rock, you know."

"Yes, I know. Geez. Dinosaurs pooped rock. I get it."

Vicki's eyes rolled. "They didn't poop rock, it turned into rock later. That's what petrified means."

"It's not what dinosaurs ate?"

Vicki slapped her forehead and glared at me with one eye half closed. I was giving her brain damage.

"Gotcha." I laughed. "I'm not that dumb. Dinosaurs ate mud, and that hardened into rock. Now let's go find Rex Rangler."

I crept off before Vicki could sigh me to death. Keeping low, I made my way alongside the back wall of the building to the edge of the dock. I peeked over the lip with one eye to see if the coast was clear. "Nobody here," I said in a whisper. "I don't see any security guards or workers. Just that package. Let's go."

I jumped up on the dock and hunkered low, crab walking behind the crate. Vicki inched in beside me.

"I think we're good," I said. "No one saw us."

Just then the crate jiggled back and forth, rattling on the concrete.

"Did you see that?" I asked.

"What? Is somebody there?"

I poked at the crate. "No, in here. It moved."

Vicki leaned in to get a better look, shaking her head. "You probably bumped it."

I knew I hadn't touched it before, but I decided to now. Up close I could see inside through the slats. Whatever was moving looked black and round like a bowling ball. It reminded me of something I'd seen recently, but I couldn't remember. Sticking my finger through an opening I gave the thing a poke.

"Weird," I said.

"What?"

"It feels wet."

I poked my finger in again. I jerked away as a blast of greenish steam hissed out. The ball rolled back and forth and banged against the sides of the crate. One corner of the crate split open.

"I think that dinosaur egg is about to hatch."

"Eggs don't give off steam," Vicki said.

"Have you ever seen a dinosaur egg hatch?"

"No, but . . ."

"Ha!"

Vicki scowled, but didn't answer. Score one for me, *Miss Know-it-all*.

I pulled the corner of the crate away to get a better look. The ball was so black it could have been a bottomless pit. I couldn't resist touching it again.

"Careful," Vicki said.

"I know what I'm doing." I plunged my hand in.

It felt like dipping my hand into the washing machine and waiting for it to start spinning. My wrist vanished. I tried to jerk it out, but the ball yanked and in a flash my whole arm slipped inside.

The thing was trying to eat me! It had to be a dinosaur egg.

Vicki let out a tiny shriek and grabbed me around the neck. I felt my throat crushing under her grip, but my arm slowly emerged from the ball as she pulled. A second later I shot free, flopping onto my back.

I bolted up and checked my arm to make sure everything had made it out okay. Five fingers, I hadn't been eaten.

Beep, beep, beeeeeeep. My ecto-meter! The screen flashed like a lightning storm, and it was ringing. A message popped onto the screen.

Vicki leaned over my shoulder. "Are you getting a signal?"

"Yeah," I said. "It's a message."

"A message? From who?"

"I don't know."

We both watched as the message scrolled out, one letter at a time.

H-E-L-P.

CHAPTER ELEVEN

IT WORKS!

Vicki and I sat on the Dino Barn loading dock, both staring at the green line on my ecto-meter as it jumped up and down across the screen. Just below it a message ran, spelling the same word over and over.

H-E-L-P--H-E-L-P--H-E-L-P--H-E-L-P--H-E-L-P

"It works!" I pumped my fist. "My ecto-meter works! The ghosts are in there."

"Inside that thing?" Vicki gasped, leaning in for a closer look at the steaming bowling ball. She squinted and stuck her finger out, but didn't touch it. "Let me see your ecto-meter."

I handed it to her and she pushed some buttons.

"Don't lose the signal," I said, watching her fiddle with the controls. "Ectoplasm dissipates pretty fast."

"It's showing a number now: 599-7890? What's that mean?"

"That shows up all the time. It's an error code. It's the wavy line that's important, and the message."

"Looks like a phone number to me," Vicki said. "Isn't this just an old phone with an ectoplasmic chip stuffed into it?"

"No. Maybe. So?"

"So somebody's texting you."

She handed the ecto-meter back and I gave it a shake. Not again. Did Vicki always have to be right? I gave it another look. A lump rose in my throat. I'd seen that same number over and over, but now I finally recognized it. It was Grandma's old phone number.

How could I have missed that? All this time she was trying to contact me and I didn't know. A pit grew in my stomach. How much time had I wasted?

"It's from my grandma. That's her number! She's in there! We have to get her out." My heart thundered like a jet.

Vicki stared at the black hole, frowning. "Trey, if you're right, do you know what this means?"

"It means we have to get my grandma out of this ball."

I'd found her, and I couldn't wait any longer. I was going to see Grandma again! I was really going to see her, just like when she was alive. "Come on, help me pry it open." I reached over to wrestle the rest of the crate away.

"Wait." Vicki pulled my hand back. "Of course we have to save your grandma. But it means something else. It also means that Rex Rangler is the ghostnapper."

I froze. "What? That can't be true. He's a good guy."

Vicki shook her head. "It all makes sense. He's tearing down those old haunted buildings like the movie theater, paving over the cemetery, and building a ghost museum. It has to be him. He's putting real ghosts into Ghostville."

I didn't believe her. Rex was my favorite TV-show host, my hero. My dad's boss. It couldn't be him.

"You're just saying that because you don't like him. Because he's tearing down those old houses you love."

But I loved them too. At least one. Grandma's house.

"Think about it, Trey. Why would this thing be here if it wasn't Rangler's?"

"Maybe he doesn't know," I said. "Maybe he thinks like I did, that ghosts are just ectoplasmic remnants and not real people."

"Maybe," Vicki said. "But he's still the one kidnapping them."

My head hurt. I couldn't just sit here and argue. I had to do something. I pulled the rest of the crate apart and leaned in over the ball. It steamed and wiggled.

"What are you doing? Don't get too close. It might not be safe."

"I have to find out for sure if Grandma is in there."

"No!" Vicki grabbed my arm.

I took a deep breath and shook her loose. Vicki had her petitions, and I had Grandma. "I'm standing up for what *I* believe in." Then I shoved my head into the ball.

The last thing I heard was Vicki shouting, "Why don't you return the message?"

Now she tells me.

* * *

At first everything went black. I had fallen into a bottomless pit. Then I thought I might be in outer space, except there were no stars. My skin crawled as I tumbled head over heels. I couldn't tell up from down. I was moving so fast I had to be billions of miles away, falling through a portal into another universe.

My head spun like a top and my stomach jumped into

my mouth. After what seemed like hours the blackness switched to a cloudy gray like the middle of a rain cloud. Then, like opening my eyes in the morning, the fog disappeared and I could see again. I was standing alone on a staircase. I looked around and saw that the steps led up to another staircase that ran in a different direction, upside down. And it connected to more steps running sideways into more stairs which ran into more stairs . . . on and on and on with no end.

I whacked my head on the flight coming down from above. That was sure to leave a bump. Rubbing my wound I crouched down and managed to get to the top without cracking my face again. The weirdest part was when I reached the last stair I flipped over and was standing straight up, but on a connecting staircase. I ran to the bottom and turned upside down again. No matter where I climbed or which steps I took, I always ended up in the place I started. I liked the blackness better.

"Hello?" I called. "Is anybody here? Grandma?"

Out of the blue dozens of fuzzy shapes materialized, misty and glowing like fireflies in smoke. I blinked and the room filled with dozens of people. Some stood around me, their eyes glaring, while others were upside down or at weird angles on different steps. They all stared and pointed.

I tried to back away, but I only switched direction and ended up surrounded by another group of blurry people. They all had a kind of whitish-gray look. Some shimmered and I could see through them to the person behind. They had to be ghosts.

The nearest spirit, a woman in a pink bathrobe, scowled wide-eyed at me. She held a tiny drooling poodle with ribbons dangling from its ears and a bow around its neck. "Why did you bring us here? Foo-Foo doesn't like it here." Foo-Foo snapped and barked. I backed into another ghost. He clawed at me but his fingers passed right through me as if I wasn't there.

I ran and tripped, falling straight through another ghost who'd swung a fist at my head. Stumbling, I dashed down the stairs, passing through every ghost on the way. They all cried out as I zoomed through their insides. But there was no place to go. The stairs all wound back on themselves and the ghosts were everywhere.

Voices called out from all directions, filling my ears

and rattling my teeth. "Let us go! Free us! We want to go home!"

I threw my hands over my ears, but the noise seeped in just like their bodies passed through me. I couldn't get away.

"I didn't bring you here! It wasn't me!"

Dozens of pale fingers pointed their accusations at me. "Where's Wethermerry? What have you done with him?"

"Nothing. He sent me here," I said.

"Let us go!"

No one listened. I hadn't cried to my grandma for help in years, but this seemed like a good time. "Grandma! It's me, Trey! Help!!!"

Just like that the crowd went quiet. The ghosts kept staring, but everyone stopped talking.

"Are you Trey?" the bathrobed woman asked.

I nodded.

Spinning and dropping her dog she cried, "It's him. It's Trey! He's here! Trey's here!" She reached out and put her hand on my face. Her fingers passed right through my nose. "She said you'd come, that you'd help us."

The pink lady stepped aside and the crowed parted. A misty shape walked toward me, solidifying until it looked like a woman with curly gray hair and glasses. She smiled big and wide. "Trey, dear. You got my text."

CATCHING UP

Grandma.

I ran up and hugged her. I hadn't seen her in two years and all I wanted was to sit on her lap again and have her read me a story even though I was too big.

I flopped right through her and bounced down the stairs like a lopsided football.

"Careful, dear," Grandma said. "I'm not as solid as I used to be." She bent over to help me up, but that didn't work any better than my hug.

She sat down beside me. "Oh, Trey, I'm so glad to see you. I told everyone that my brave boy would come to help us, and here you are. You're looking so grown-up."

For some reason, even though I couldn't touch her, Grandma still smelled the same as always. Kind of a mixture of roses and that sticky hard candy she kept in a bowl that even I couldn't choke down.

I had so many questions, but something nagged at me even more.

"I . . . I'm sorry I didn't go to your funeral, Grandma. I . . ." I looked away. She always said I was so brave, how could I tell her I was too scared to go?

She smiled and tilted her head. "Don't worry about that, Trey. I wasn't there myself."

"Really?"

"Oh heavens no, funerals are no fun. I sat in the car with my grandson, holding his hand. I felt so much braver with your help, just like now."

I remembered that day. I'd thought I'd imagined holding her hand. "You were there?"

"Of course."

"Did it hurt?" I asked. "You know, when you died?"

"Not that I remember. More like falling asleep."

"I'm glad," I said. I didn't want to think she'd suffered. "Who brought you here?" I crossed my fingers and hoped Vicki was wrong and that it wasn't Rangler.

"It was the strangest thing," Grandma said. "I was at home, looking through some old photos after the funeral. Then out of the blue these men burst in, beep-beeping everywhere. The next thing I knew I was trapped here with all these nice people."

I gasped. "They tore your house down a year ago."

Grandma put her hand over her mouth. "Has it been that long? No wonder you look so big and grown-up. I guess I lost track. Time seems to stand still, and since I'm not getting any older I don't watch the clock too much."

"How did you know I'd come?" I asked. "You . . . you can't see me all the time can you?" I started worrying that she'd been watching while Hardy was getting me into trouble. "'Cause I'm sorry about the glue on the seats."

Grandma smiled. "Don't worry, dear, I only haunted you that once."

That was lucky, because we did the glue thing a lot.

"Who else would I call but my brave grandson?" She smiled and tried to touch my cheek. "You always said you were going to find a real ghost. And I was lucky I had this." She reached into her pocket and pull out her phone. It looked just like the one I'd transformed into my ecto-meter. We were probably still on the same family plan. "I texted the address to your mom, too, just in case. I'm so glad you finally answered. I haven't paid the bill so I was a little worried."

"That's why mom took us to the wrong place," I said.

It made sense now. Grandma had been sending me clues all along. "I talked to Wethermerry. He told me you'd been kidnapped."

"Isn't he a wonderful man? So concerned about all of us."

"He's a little weird," I said.

Grandma chuckled. "Smokes too much, too. But very nice."

"How can you use that?" I pointed at her phone. "Your hands go right through everything else."

Grandma shrugged. "For some reason we ghosts can use anything we were holding, or wearing, when we died. Luckily it works with clothes, too." She smoothed her pant suit. "I really hate this thing. It was a present from your mother. I hope they didn't bury me in it."

I looked down at the floor and wondered if she ever liked my presents either. But bugs glued to a paper plate are way cooler than a green pants suit. Maybe she could borrow some different clothes once we'd gotten out of here. That reminded me of something else. With her house torn down, where would she live?

I'd have to take her home with me. Mom had always

wanted her to live with us anyway. And ghosts didn't need that much room so I was sure Dad wouldn't mind. We'd all be together again. I smiled at my brilliant plan.

"Come on, Grandma. We're leaving." I looked around. I was so excited to see her I'd forgotten that there wasn't any way out, just the stairways to nowhere. I didn't know how to get home any more than the ghosts did.

"We better give this a little more thought." Grandma smiled. "I wouldn't want you to miss any school on my account."

I tried to remember how I'd gotten here, but that was just a blur. I didn't know if I was inside that ball on the loading dock or in another dimension.

"There's no egress."

Grandma clapped her hands. "Oh my! Egress! What a wonderful word. The things they teach in school these days."

"Actually I learned it — "

Suddenly my middle squeezed like a vice. A tornado swirled around me and I stretched into spaghetti just like Wethermerry. Except he was a ghost and didn't mind.

"Grandma! Help!"

She reached out her hands, but they flowed right through me. In another second Grandma and the rest of the ghosts shrank in the distance and the blackness returned. Something was pulling me away.

After a minute of flying across the universe I opened my eyes and shook my head. Wrapped around my waist and staring me straight in the face was a gigantic, monstrous, horrible . . .

"Vicki?"

"Why did you put your head in there? You got stuck. I had to pull you out."

"What do you mean? I was inside this totally other dimension."

"No you weren't," Vicki said. "You put your face in the ball and sat there for a minute. I heard someone coming, so I yanked you out."

"No way. I saw my grandma. All the ghosts are inside. We have to get them out."

"We'll have to come back later." Vicki tugged on my arm and I followed her jerking head toward a door leading inside the building. The knob turned and the door cracked open. Then the tip of a giant mustache appeared around the edge. Right behind it flashed a dino suit, covered with Christmas lights.

"Run," Vicki whispered.

I took one last look at the black hole and promised Grandma that I'd be back, whatever it took.

CHAPTER THIRTEEN

THE REAL REX RANGLER

We slid off the Dino Barn loading dock but the door opened all the way before we could run. Hunkering below the lip of the dock I held my breath and waited. Vicki even stopped chewing her bubble gum.

I still couldn't believe Rangler was behind all the ghostnapping. Maybe it wasn't him. Maybe his lackeys wanted to impress him by capturing real ghosts. He was a big TV star, and everyone loves TV stars.

"What's that doing there?" Rangler slapped at a guard on his right, all muscles and hairy arms. He was the same one who'd gotten me in trouble the day before. "What idiot left that sitting outside in the open?"

Hey! He was talking about my dad!

"Some numbskull leaves our top-secret project on the porch? Morons! I work with morons!"

The guard nodded blankly while he scanned the dock, looking out from behind his sunglasses. "I'll check into it."

"Be sure you do," Rangler said with a sneer. "Or you'll be looking for work. I don't tolerate screwups. No one else in the world will have real ghosts in their amusement park. Can you imagine the crowds, and all that money? We can't risk anyone finding a stray containment unit lying around, giving away our secrets."

"Did you hear that?" Vicki poked me and whispered in my ear. "He said 'real ghosts.' He is behind it."

I swallowed the lump in my throat. Vicki was right. Rex Rangler was a ghostnapper.

"I thought I heard someone." One of the guards took three steps toward us and peered down. I scrunched under the overhang as far as I could. Vicki held her breath. He seemed to stare right over us, and Vicki started to shake, her lips quivering.

The guard took a sniff. "Smells like gum."

Vicki's eyes bugged out and with a giant swallow she choked down her bubble gum.

"Never mind that," Rangler said. "Get this crate inside."

The guard turned away and walked back to the door by Rangler.

Vicki let out a breath and rubbed her throat. "That was close. Let's listen and maybe he'll tell us how to get the ghosts out."

"That only happens in the movies," I said. "Real bad guys aren't dumb enough to tell you how to defeat them."

"Get this thing inside," Rangler said. "And be careful not to touch it. Once we empty it into the ectoplasmic projector we'll be able to bring the ghosts out for display anytime we want." He rubbed his hands together with glee. "When the permanent containment unit is operating they won't be able to escape. I'm glad we tested it at the old museum. It's a work of genius, if I do say so myself."

He wiggled his eyebrows, which were almost as big as his mustache. They looked like wings and he was ready for takeoff.

Vicki grinned.

"Well, *sometimes* movies are like real life," I said.

"Dude!"

Vicki and I both spun around at the sound of a bike skidding to a stop behind us.

"Trey, man. I've been looking for you. Want your

drink?" Hardy hefted a turbo-bladder-blaster over his head. Then he frowned at Vicki. "Didn't you leave?"

It only took Rangler and the guards a second to figure out this kid with the monster-sized drinking cup wasn't talking to them. The toe of a blinking boot appeared over my head.

I shot off like rubber-band gun, but ran head-on into a security guard, smushing my nose on his plastic badge. A guy named Brick scooped me up by my arms.

"Let me go!" Vicki had made it a little further than I had, but the other guard ran her down before she could round the building. Kicking her legs and flailing, she struggled as he carried her under an arm. The same guard dragged Hardy with his other hand. He'd spilled his drink all over the parking lot.

"Dude! I paid four bucks for that Watermelon-Whizzer. You owe me."

Rex Rangler stared at me while Brick pinned my arms at my sides. My feet hung a foot off the ground.

"Do I know you?" He squinted and furrowed his brow.

"No."

"Wait, wait." He looked back and forth between me and Vicki. "You're that kid . . . those kids, with all the questions about ghosts, aren't you? Come back to see for yourselves?"

Rangler waved at the guy holding Vicki and Hardy to let them down. Hardy stared at his drink-stained shirt looking like he might try to suck it clean with his straw.

"You're just curious kids," Rangler said. "No crime in sneaking in without a ticket."

I let out a sigh, but I was still being squeezed by Brick.

"Well, there is a law, technically. It's called trespassing. But I guess we can overlook that, this time."

Brick dropped me like a rock.

"Cool suit," Hardy said.

"You have an eye for fine clothing, young man." Rangler admired his own outfit. The tiny LED lights flickered against the rhinestones outlining the dinosaurs. "Sorry for the mistake, but you can't be too careful. We've had a few folks who couldn't wait until we opened to see what was inside. Ghostville promises to be a revolution in ghostly/paranormal entertainment, and there are unscrupulous people out there who'd pay lots of money to discover my secrets." He glanced sideways as if someone was listening.

I bit my lip. I couldn't let him know that I'd heard anything.

"We just wanted to see inside," Vicki said. "You know, dinosaurs."

Good job, Vicki. Maybe we could get out of here without giving up *our* secrets.

But there was still Hardy. Luckily he didn't know what was going on, so of course he couldn't blow it.

"Trey," Hardy said. "Did you tell him about those two ghosts at the museum, and ask for help finding your grandma and the other kidnapped ghosts?"

Rangler went stiff. First his mustache bolted out like it had springs. Then his eyebrow wings started flapping. He looked like one of those old biplanes.

"Kidnapped! What do you mean, kidnapped?"

"Huh?" I said. "What?" I took a quick look at Hardy like I didn't know what he was talking about. "Um . . . what?"

"Geez, dude," Hardy said. "You didn't forget about your grandma's ghost already, did you?"

Thanks, Hardy.

Rangler grabbed my arm. His whole body shook. He seemed to be noticing for the first time that the crate was broken. "You appear to be the instigator here. What did you see? What two ghosts at the old museum?"

I grunted. "Nothing."

"Chill," Hardy said. "Tell him, Trey."

I leaned away from Rangler's mustache. It threatened to poke my eyes out if he got any closer.

"What two ghosts?" he asked again.

I kept quiet.

Rangler sniffed. "Perhaps I should call the police, see what they think about trespassing kids."

"I thought you said you'd overlook us not having tickets," I said.

"I lied."

"No." Vicki tried to jerk her arm free. "I don't want to go to jail."

"Then tell me about those two ghosts," Rangler said. "What do you know?"

"Nothing," I said. "Let us go."

"Hey, brush-face," Hardy said.

Rangler turned with a snarl. Hardy whipped his dino poop out of his pocket and splatted the ghostnapper smack between the eyes. The goo slithered over his face, sticking to his wing-like eyebrows.

Rangler yelped and yanked at the blob. Tiny bits pulled loose, covered with hair. The glop attacked his face like zombie bubble gum. I kicked my guard in the knee, grabbed Vicki's hand, and ran.

"Let's get out of here!"

Hardy was ahead of me. Without a gallon of soda in his hand he moved pretty fast. We bolted past his bike and hit the trail, rounding the building and racing to the front parking lot where hundreds of people were still lined up to get inside the Dino Barn. In a few seconds we lost ourselves in the crowd, ducking down and pretending to be with all the other kids waiting for tickets. Rangler stopped at the corner of the building. I guess he didn't want to be seen chasing three kids with poop on his face.

Once we'd stopped running I slapped Hardy on the back, "Wow, good one. That dino poop really worked."

Hardy frowned. "Those guys spilled my drink and now they have my dino poop. I should get a free ticket."

Even Vicki seemed happy with Hardy. "I'll buy you one when we save Trey's grandma and Rangler's in jail."

Hardy stared at her for a second. I think he was still wondering why I was hanging with Vicki, or maybe imagining what she'd look like with goo stuck to her face. He shrugged. "Whatever."

Hardy had to leave his bike behind, so he sat on my handle bars on the way home. My bike creaked and groaned under the extra weight and I couldn't see around him. Luckily I only nicked two trees and a parked car. No real damage. To me anyway.

Once we were out of sight of the Dino Barn Vicki pulled up next to me. "Rangler knows about Wethermerry and Mr. Greensocks. We should go back and warn them before he shows up."

I nodded. I didn't want Rangler to snatch anyone else. And maybe Wethermerry could give us some clues about how to get Grandma out of that black hole.

"So is she going to hang around with us all the time now?" Hardy asked as I weaved and wobbled down the street while checking over my shoulder for any pursuit. Vicki pulled ahead and I hoped she couldn't hear us.

"Uh, yeah, I guess. She's not that bad. I'd never have found my grandma without her. So she's okay. But don't tell her that, it's a secret."

"That's a secret I can keep." Hardy scowled.

Vicki dropped back next to us and leaned over toward me. "I have secret." She whispered so Hardy couldn't hear. "I think you're okay, too."

CHAPTER FOURTEEN

BEING A GHOST

After we'd escaped from Rex Rangler and his goon squad, Hardy, Vicki and I raced home to come up with a new plan. Halfway back Vicki's phone buzzed.

"But Mom," Vicki said. "I told you I was with a friend. His name's Trey . . .. No, his mom knows me . . . okay." She clicked off her phone. "I have to go home. Sorry. I'll convince my mom by tomorrow that you're nice. Then I can help you again."

"Don't bother," Hardy said.

I jabbed him and nodded at Vicki. "Okay. Make sure you do."

Vicki grinned. "I will." After a few more blocks she turned off for her house.

"Finally," Hardy said over his shoulder as Vicki rode away. "We don't need her. We can find your grandma by ourselves."

"Why don't you want her to come?"

Hardy rolled his eyes. "Because, dude."

"Because why? I told you she was okay. I wish you'd stop teasing her."

"Stop teasing her?" Hardy elbowed me. "That's what we do. She's not one of us. We're a team. We don't need anyone else."

Hardy was right; we did everything as a team, especially get into trouble. We stuck up for each other. When Grandma died he didn't even mind when I sat in his basement without talking and didn't want to play video games. It was always me and Hardy and no one else. But Vicki was different. I didn't know why.

I slapped him on the back. "Just stop teasing her, okay?"

"Whatever, dude," Hardy said, looking away. We rode the rest of the way home in silence.

* * *

Dad took Mom and me out for pizza and then ice cream that night. Dad seemed way happier than I'd seen him in forever.

"Ham and pineapple, buddy?" Dad asked. "Your favorite, right?"

"Yeah. No rice."

The pizza was really good and I ate like a pig. Halfway through my seventh slice my stomach stabbed at me and I started feeling guilty. I thought back to when Grandma used to come over on pizza night. One time she told me how she'd met Grandpa over a pizza. She stuck pepperoni to her nose. "This was how I got Grandpa to notice me on our first date," she'd said, doing a dance. Grandma loved pizza.

I wondered if Vicki liked pizza.

Mom must have noticed me stop in the middle of my slice. "Trey, are you okay? Getting full?"

"No. Just needed to breathe." I scarfed down the rest of the slice so fast I got sauce burn. I didn't want Mom or Dad asking me how I felt or trying to stick a flashlight in my mouth. And the faster I ate the easier it was to keep both Grandma and Vicki out of my thoughts. I ordered the extra-humungo chocolate fudge caramel sundae with nuts to ease my pain.

"Slow down," Mom said. "I guess you must be feeling better. At least until you notice how much you've eaten."

Dad belched. "Can't have too much of a good thing."

Mom rolled her eyes and Dad winked at me. He knew she disliked his deep, resonant burps, but they always made me laugh. He hadn't burped at the table in months. I missed them.

I opened my mouth to let out Belchzilla, the blast of the century.

"Don't you dare, mister," Mom said, laughing. "That's what I get for having two boys." She shook her head, but I could see her huge smile. I really liked hearing her laugh again.

Mom was right though. I couldn't sleep that night because my stomach felt like I'd swallowed a box of boulders. I laid awake thinking of those crazy stairs and Grandma trapped in some weird alternate-dimension bowling ball. The more I thought about that, the more my gut ached. What if I couldn't get her out? What if I couldn't stop Rangler and he succeeded in putting her into his amusement park? I was so happy to see her again, what if the next time she was a display, like those robot dinosaurs? I tapped out a text, but there was no answer. I hid under my pillow until the sun rose, then I got up before Dad left for work.

"Where are you off to so early? Looking for ghosts again?" he asked me.

I shrugged and tried not to look scared. I didn't know how to tell him that his boss was a ghostnapper. "Just hanging with Hardy."

Dad furrowed his brow and stared at me for a moment. What had he noticed? I smiled a little.

"You look like you swallowed a bug."

"Just a pizza."

"Yeah, it didn't sit too well with me either." He grinned and rubbed his stomach. "I guess we need to wean ourselves off the rice more slowly. Well, I'm going to work. Hopefully I won't always have to go on weekends. When I get some time we'll do something fun. I'll take you to Ghostville when it opens. I'm sure I'll get an employee discount. Doesn't that sound good?"

I choked up and had to turn away to hide my eyes. Thinking about walking into Ghostville with Mom and Dad and seeing Grandma on display like a circus freak left me short of breath. Would they even notice it was her? Would anyone suspect that Rangler had enslaved real ghosts? I swallowed my tears. "Yeah. Great. Can't wait."

Dad wrapped his arm around my shoulder. "I can't tell you how excited I am about this job. I know it's been hard for you, too. First losing your grandma, then having to eat rice all the time. But things really will be better from now on." He put his finger under my chin and tilted my head up to look at him. "Sorry if I've been a bit of a drudge lately. I'll make it up to you."

"That's okay. I understand."

"You know you can talk to me about anything, right?"

"Yeah. I know." I almost told him everything right then, but it would have spoiled his new job.

"Have an awesome day, buddy."

"You too, Dad."

After Dad drove off in his Rangler Enterprises truck I met Vicki at the corner. I guessed she'd convinced her mom that I was safe. Hardy wasn't there. He'd always been there before.

"Hi, Vicki." I gave her a little wave.

"Hi, Trey." She smiled back, wiggling her fingers at me.

I didn't know why, but my hand reached up on its own and tried to straighten my hair. Maybe *I was haunted*.

My mouth went off on its own, too. "Um . . . do you like pizza?"

"Yeah. I love pizza."

"Me too," I said.

Vicki grinned. "Ready to go?"

I looked around to see if Hardy would show. The street was empty. It was just me and Vicki. "I guess."

I was climbing on my bike when I heard a shout from across the street. "Dude, what's with you? Were you going without me?"

I waited for Hardy to ride up the driveway. "I didn't think you'd show." I wanted him to come, but I was still mad.

Hardy grunted and looked sideways at Vicki. "No, I'm coming. You need someone who knows what they're doing."

"No teasing," I said.

"Whatever."

We took off for the old museum to warn our ghost friends that Rangler knew about them. I tried to ride next to Vicki, but Hardy kept cutting in between. He had borrowed his little sister Teko's bike and whacked his knees on the handle bars.

"At least she took off the training wheels." I laughed as Hardy struggled to keep riding straight. "That's a cute basket though, and I really love those frilly things on the handles. You look totally fast."

"Shut up!"

It was Sunday and without much traffic we made it to the museum pretty fast. We ditched our bikes by the curb. The old building was still abandoned, no cars in the lot and not a sign of anyone. I creaked open the doors and we slipped in.

"Mr. Lewis?" Vicki called out. "Mr. Greensocks? Are you there?"

The place was dark except for the always flickering red neon *Egress* sign.

"Oh cool," Hardy said. "Egress. I saw one in a movie. It's some kind of giant people-eating bird with a sharp beak and octopus arms. It had rocket-powered farts, too." He shot off, following the arrow and in a second disappeared around the corner.

Rocket-powered farts? I wished.

"Should we tell him?" Vicki asked.

"He'll be back."

Running up to the second floor, I searched for any signs of the ghosts. I checked my ecto-meter. It was flat-lined. Were we too late?

"Wethermerry! Where are you?"

No answer.

"Where could they be?" Vicki chomped on a new piece of gum. She chewed harder when she was nervous. She tried to blow a bubble again, and this time the wad landed on my foot. I didn't even mind.

"Please pick that up and throw it away," a voice behind me said. "No gum allowed in the theater."

I whipped around to find Mr. Greensocks's familiar paleness floating a foot off the ground. He was pointing at my shoe.

"Oh good. We were looking for you. We found where the ghosts are but we don't know how to get them out. I thought you might know. Oh, and Rangler's coming, so we have to hide you, too. Where's Wethermerry?"

Mr. Greensocks stared at me, shaking his head and pointing at my foot.

"Did you hear me? Rangler's coming."

"The gum, if you please," Mr. Greensocks said. "In the trash."

He was pretty fussy about stepping in something for a guy whose feet didn't touch the ground. I leaned over to grab the gum and knocked heads with Vicki. "I got it."

"Thanks."

Her fingers touched mine just as I picked up the gum. My hand tingled. I got confused for a second and stuffed the gum in my pocket. It squished into my allowance money. Vicki giggled.

Satisfied that I wasn't a litterer, the ghost of the old theater owner lifted up toward the rafters like a puff of smoke. He misted right through the ceiling and vanished.

"I wish I could do that," I said. "Except without the having to be dead first thing."

Vicki smiled and nodded. "You never told me about your grandma. Is she okay?"

"Well, she didn't like being held prisoner, and inside

that ball was really weird. It was all stairs leading nowhere, just back into each other. She really wanted out."

"What's it like being dead?"

My chest went cold. Whenever I thought about Grandma being dead I felt like I was stuck in a freezer. But it seemed different now. She wasn't just someone I used to know and love. Sure, she was trapped in that weird every-dimensional place, but I didn't think of her as dead anymore, just a little different. Kind of hazy and transparent, but still Grandma.

I shrugged. "I'm not sure. She didn't talk about it."

"Where will the ghosts go when we free them?" Vicki asked. "All those old houses are torn down." She looked up at the ceiling. Greensocks hadn't come back. "Maybe they'll just move on."

"Move on?" The cold came back. "What do you mean? I told my grandma she could live with us at my house. I'm sure my mom and dad won't mind."

"Are you sure?" Vicki asked. "I think most ghosts move on after a while. That's why they're so hard to find. Their spirits don't stay here for very long after they die."

My gut dropped. I'd just found Grandma again. I didn't want to lose her a second time.

"I don't think so." I shook my head. "She'll want to stay with me."

Wouldn't she?

Vicki stared at me for a moment, not saying anything. She nodded. "Yeah, she probably will." Then she turned away. I saw a small tear run down her cheek. Her voice kind of cracked a little as she asked, "Did you . . . did you see anyone else in there?"

"Yeah. There were a bunch of ghosts. Some weird pink lady with a freaky dog, and lots of others. They were kind of creepy at first. But I got used to it."

"Was there a man there, in . . . in a uniform? Like the army?" Her eyes got really big and wet.

I scratched my head, trying to remember. Besides the pink lady and Grandma, everyone else was a blur. "No, I didn't see anyone from the army. Why?"

"I just thought . . . oh, no reason. Just wondering."

There was something Vicki wasn't telling me. Who was she looking for?

"Are you sure?" I asked.

She looked at the ground and started to mumble, sniffing and wiping at her eyes, "Well, I . . ."

Just then I heard a whoop from the first floor. We ran downstairs and saw Wethermerry near the ceiling, drifting down like a cloud, waving his coonskin hat around his head. "Yee-haw! You're back! And you found that blasted jail. Let's go catch us a ghostnapper!"

CHAPTER FIFTEEN

PRISON BREAK

Vicki and I had found Wethermerry before Rangler got to him. Hardy was outside. He'd fallen for the old egress trick. I raced toward the door, stopping just before I opened it. I glanced back at Wethermerry.

"You'll get turned into spaghetti," I said.

Wethermerry grinned. "Been doing some investigating. I think I've figured out how it works."

Just then the door flew open.

"Dude," Hardy said, stumbling his way back inside. "There's no egress, just the exit."

A tornado blew up around my feet and Hardy's hair stood on end. Wethermerry swirled like he'd been flushed down a toilet. I covered my eyes from the dust, and Wethermerry and Mr. Greensocks slowly whipped into noodles.

"Close it!" I pointed at Hardy, shouting. He slammed the door and the wind stopped. The two ghosts regained their regular shapes.

Hardy grabbed my shoulder and spun me around. "Dude, are those the ghosts? They're so awesome!"

I nodded. "The guy in the leather is the town founder, Wethermerry Lewis."

"No way. I've heard that name before."

"We live in Lewisville."

"So?"

"And we go to school at Wethermerry Lewis Elementary."

A light flashed on in Hardy's eyes. "That's him? That's the guy?"

"I know. Cool, huh?"

Wethermerry floated beside us, a shadow under a hat. He had an old musket slung over one shoulder and a jagged, ghostly knife big enough to be a sword strapped to his hip. He tipped his hat to Hardy. "Nice to meet you."

"That's so cool," Hardy said.

"I thought you had the egress figured out." I said to Wethermerry.

He frowned. "Let me check one more thing." Wethermerry wafted back up toward the ceiling, right into the egress sign.

I looked around for Vicki. She was trailing behind with her hands in her pockets, staring at the floor. I walked back over to her. There were streaks running down her face. She caught me staring and wiped her nose.

"You okay?"

"The soldier," she said. "He's my dad. I was hoping maybe he did come home from the war after all. I wanted to say good-bye."

Vicki's dad was dead? I never knew that. I thought when she said he wasn't around that her parents were divorced. She hadn't told anyone at school, even on Veterans Day when Mr. Brakenbush talked about soldiers dying in the war. But she had mentioned visiting a cemetery and that her mom didn't like ghosts because she didn't want to be reminded of something. I guess that explains why Vicki was so interested in finding ghosts with me and had asked all those questions about Grandma dying, and maybe even why she was a little weird. I'd be weird too if my dad went off to war and never came home. I'd been plenty weird after Grandma died. It's funny how people are different once you know something about them.

Sometimes they don't even seem weird anymore.

"Sorry," I said.

Vicki cracked a thin smile. "Thanks." She reached out and touched my hand for a second. I grabbed a finger. This time the tingling felt warm, too.

Wethermerry let out another whoop. I looked up and saw him twirling around the flashing sign. Drifting in and out from between the letters he popped his head through the hole in the G and winked. "I was right. This is what's been keeping us here."

"But that's just an exit sign," I said. "It's not an exit."

"Open the door."

"But . . ."

"Just open it, and look up here."

I nodded at Hardy and he pulled the door open.

I hadn't noticed before, but the sign brightened and glowed even more strongly, like glowing coals when you blow on them. And of course the ghosts got blenderized.

"That's enough!" I shouted above the wind. Hardy slammed the door.

"Looks like some kind of force field that turns on

when you open the door," I said. "That must be how that ghost prison works, too."

"That's more than I know," Wethermerry said. "But there's only one solution — break it!"

"Whoo hoo! I can do that." Hardy instantly ran to an open broom closet. Piece after piece of junk flew out and crashed at my feet. "Got it!" Hardy jumped out waving an old dented bucket and a broken mop handle.

"Here, dude." He handed me the bucket. "You try knocking it down with this, and I'll use the spear."

Vicki cleared her throat. "Is there something *I* can throw?"

"I don't know," Hardy said. "Can *girls* throw?"

"Shut up, dude." I handed Vicki the bucket. "Here, try this." I leaned over and whispered, "Your dad might be there. I didn't really look too closely. I just wanted to find my grandma."

"That's okay," she said. "I'm sure he isn't. I'm used to it now."

Hardy glared at me, shaking his head. "Dude, I don't even know you. I can't believe you've really got a girlfriend."

What was he talking about? Vicki was just my friend. "Shut up and throw your spear. We have to get out of here. Hurry!"

Hardy turned around and gripped his weapon, gritting his teeth. "Whatever."

He reached back and just like we always practiced against the side of the garage with any heavy sticks we could find, he launched it at the sign. And just like always the mop handle sailed right by, missing the glass tubes by a foot.

"Let me try again." Hardy dashed over to retrieve the stick. "I'll get it this time."

But before he could even reach his spear I saw the bucket arch out of Vicki's hand, tumble overhead and smash straight into the *E* of egress. Red sparks zinged in a giant rainbow as tiny glass pieces rained down on us.

"That's for your grandma."

I snatched up the fallen bucket and hurled it again as Hardy ducked away from the shards of glass. This time the missile brought down the rest of the sign in a big spray. Hardy plucked the glass out of his hair.

"That's for your dad."

"Mighty fine shootin', you two," Wethermerry said. "Mighty fine. Looks like we've got a man and a woman of action. Shall we go to the rescue?"

I reached for the door and slowly pulled it open. There was no wind, no sucking, no swirling, no flushing.

One prison break down, one to go.

CHAPTER SIXTEEN

ON THE RUN

Now that Vicki and I had broken the egress sign that held Wethermerry and Mr. Greensocks hostage, there was nothing to keep us from leaving the old museum where Rangler had been testing his ghost prison. We all dashed out the door, including the two ghosts who floated right beside us.

"So who is this villain holding my friends, and your dear grandmother?" Wethermerry asked. "I can't wait to get my hands on him."

"His name's Rex Rangler," Vicki said.

"Rangler, huh? Sounds like a horse thief. We used to hang horse thieves." He reached around his throat and pretended to pull, bugging his eyes and sticking out his tongue.

"We found a weird black hole at the Dino Barn with the ghosts inside it," I said. "I stuck my head in and talked to my grandma."

Wethermerry's jaw dropped. "Stuck your head in,

ya say? Well good for you. You're far braver than I. No wonder your grandmother trusts you. I'm a bit embarrassed to be hiding. Is everyone doing all right?"

I nodded. "They're all okay, but Rangler caught us. He wants to have real ghosts for a haunted museum. He's coming here to get you."

"Then let's get going. We can hang the cuss later."

The screech of tires interrupted us. A van whipped into the parking lot and squealed to a stop. Led by Brick, three of Rangler's security guards jumped out. Brick carried a long hose connected to what looked like the black hole that held Grandma.

"Whoa there." Wethermerry hovered over my head to get a better look. "I've seen that thing before. I'd just as soon not get too close."

"Then we better run."

With Wethermerry flying next to my right ear, we headed behind the building to the back gate. I checked over my shoulder for the theater owner. He was still behind us, staring like a deer caught in headlights.

Brick pointed his ghost hose at Mr. Greensocks. His eyes bugged out and then his ears wiggled and flopped and what little hair he had jetted out over his face. In another second his arms and legs shot straight forward and he was sucked into the hose. It was a ghost vacuum cleaner.

"They got him!" Vicki screamed, turning around. "We have to go back."

"We can't help him now." Wethermerry waved us on. "Keep moving."

I'm a pretty fast runner, and Hardy isn't too bad either. I was afraid we might lose Vicki, so I slowed down, but she blew right past me. She's a much better runner than bubble-gum-bubble blower.

"Where are we going?" Hardy leaned on his knees and panted after we'd made it out of the parking lot.

I looked at Vicki. "Back to the Dino Barn to free my grandma," I said. "That's what we came for."

"They'll be waiting for us," Hardy said.

"It's the only thing we can do," Vicki said. "There isn't anyone left to ask for help. We have to do it ourselves."

The van rumbled around the corner. I saw Brick at the wheel, grinning behind his sunglasses. He loved his job too much.

"Down that alley," I said, pointing. It looked narrow and crowded with trash cans. Hardy dashed in first and I ducked in behind Vicki. Wethermerry flew over my head. The van spun its tires and screeched after us.

I pushed over a trash can to block the entrance, but the van didn't even slow down. Brick crashed right through in a spray of wet paper and rotten food. Up ahead a chain-link fence blocked the end of the passage.

"Oh no." Vicki rattled the fence. "We're trapped."

I looked around for another way out, but there were no doors and no way around the fence. The van slowed to a crawl and inched its way toward us.

"There's no egress." I liked saying egress.

"Yeah, we sure could use some exploding farts right now," Hardy said.

"What?"

"It would cut right through the fence."

"Oh, good idea."

Wethermerry wafted down from over my head. He straightened his coonskin cap, fluffed his beard, whipped his musket off his shoulder, and attached his wicked knife to the barrel as a bayonet. He pointed it toward the van. "It's about time I lived up to my reputation as a fighter." He pulled back the hammer on his gun. "No more running or hiding while my friends suffer. You kids climb over that fence while I hold them varmints off. I'll give you enough time to get clear and then follow after you."

"Wait. Will that gun work?" I asked. "I know my grandma's phone sends texts, but ghosts can't touch anyone."

Wethermerry grinned. "Let's find out." Then he let out a wild screeching whoop and zoomed off down the alley. A roar and a flash and a puff of smoke erupted from his rifle.

Brick and the other guards, who'd climbed out of the van by now, flinched and dived back behind the opened doors for cover while Wethermerry reloaded.

Ghost guns did work.

"That'll teach you to mess with the man who founded this town! Now go on! Run!"

I jumped up onto the fence, gripping the rough metal and wedging my feet into the small diamond-shaped openings. It was a tight fit, but I got enough of a foothold to start climbing. Hardy was already near the top and Vicki raced up right behind me. Then I heard Brick shout, "Wait a minute. He's a ghost. He can't shoot us."

Ghost guns don't work.

In another second Brick dived back into the van and snagged his ghost vacuum. "You won't get away this time." He aimed the hose at Wethermerry. My ghost friend was still ramming another bullet down the barrel of his gun when he looked up in amazement. First his furry hat whipped off his head, and then the musket flew out of his hand. In a blinding swirl Wethermerry twisted and spun.

"Run!" he said one last time. Then he was sucked away.

I stopped at the top of the fence, one leg hanging over. Without Wethermerry, I had no idea how to free Grandma.

"Hurry, dude." Hardy dropped down the other side of the fence and landed on the pavement.

"But we need him."

"They'll get you, too." I'd never seen Hardy this careful about me before.

Vicki sat on the top of the fence with me. She reached out and gave me a small shove. My feet slipped but I managed to grab hold with one hand. Vicki had pushed me to my death, again, just like at the elevator at the old museum.

"Hey. Watch it."

"Sorry. But you have to save your grandma." Then she turned and jumped.

"What are you doing? They'll get you. I need you."

"You can do this, Trey. I have to see for myself if my dad is in there."

Before I could move Vicki balled her fists and dashed straight at the still-sucking ghost-vacuum. I hoped that it wouldn't work on a real person, but in the blink of an eye Vicki's feet whipped off the ground and she twirled and stretched, her arms flailing. In another second she'd vanished.

Hardy grabbed my arm and pulled me down the next street. We ran until we couldn't breathe anymore. We'd lost Brick and the other guards.

And Vicki.

I hoped she would find her dad.

CHAPTER SEVENTEEN

G-G-GIRLFRIEND

Vicki was gone, sucked into the ghost vacuum by Brick, Rangler's number-one thug. Hardy and I ran. We were a dozen blocks away when I spotted the Rangler Enterprises van again. I pulled Hardy down behind a parked car, interrupting his after-kidnapping snack.

"That was my last candy bar." He stared at his candy floating in the gutter. I think he was tearing up.

I pointed at the van, but Brick drove right by without looking. I guessed he had what he wanted. He'd captured Wethermerry and Vicki, and I had no way of getting them back. My stomach ached and I couldn't breathe. I was just getting to know her.

I sat down on the curb and felt something sticky. Chocolate and nuts, just what I needed. I didn't even bother wiping it off my butt. Vicki had come up with all the ideas. I just stuck my head into things. Or sat on them.

"I'm sorry, Vicki," I said to myself. "Please help her, Grandma."

Hardy kicked my foot. "You coming? We have to get to the Dino Barn and rescue your grandma."

I grunted and stared at my feet. I couldn't rescue anybody. I'd screwed up everything. I was much better at getting people captured.

"Come on." Hardy gave me a shove. "Let's move."

"Since when are you so helpful?" I glared at him.

Hardy frowned and stared back at me. "Since always. We're a team, remember?"

"A team! Vicki was the only one I could count on. You were too busy being a jerk."

"Me? You're the one who ran off with a girl."

"Ran off? What are you talking about?"

Hardy rolled his eyes and then glared at me. "You left me so you could hang with her. That's not cool, dude."

"I asked you to come. Why did you have to be such an idiot?"

"Is that why you're hanging with her, because you think I'm stupid and she's smart?"

I stared at Hardy. What was wrong with him? "No, dude. But Vicki is cool too. I can have more than one friend."

Hardy sighed and shook his head. "I . . . You're my only friend."

I gaped at Hardy. He'd never told me how he felt about anything before, except when I kicked him in the shins, and he told me with a punch. I guessed I had never said how I felt either. "You're still my best friend. But Vicki is my friend, too." I looked away. "Was my friend. She's gone, and it's my fault."

Hardy shook his head. "I'm still not sure why you care, but Vicki's going to be fine. Weren't you inside that thing? You got out."

"Only because Vicki was smart enough to save me."

"You're the smart one. You always come up with good ideas. Think of one now. Your grandma needs you. And so does Vicki. I don't like her, but you do, for some reason. Let's go rescue her. She already saved you."

I sat and stared, picking at the chocolate on my butt. Hardy was right. Vicki would do it for me.

But how?

Hardy held out his hand to help me up. "Buds?" he asked.

"Buds."

Just then a pickup screeched to a halt in front of us. On the door it said *Rangler Enterprises*.

"Dude, run!" Hardy jerked my arm and took off up the street. The tug pulled me off balance and I hit the sidewalk. I looked up expecting to see Brick or another of Rangler's men with that vacuum. The window on the door lowered.

"You okay, big guy?" My dad stuck his head out the window. I'd forgotten that he was working for Rangler. "Where's Hardy off to? Run out of candy?"

"Something like that."

Hardy must have seen my dad, because he showed up a few seconds later, panting. "Too much running. Need food."

I guessed it was about time I told Dad what was going on. Maybe he could figure out what to do.

"Um, Dad . . ." I scooted into the cab while Hardy shoved me and wiped his hands on my back. "There's something about this guy you work for that you should know . . ."

I told Dad everything, even about Vicki nearly pushing me over the fence. He stared, his eyes gaping open. He didn't say anything, just shook his head, even after I finished.

"You believe me, don't you? It's all true, everything. I swear."

"It's true." Hardy took a bite and licked his fingers. He'd magically found a backup snack. "I didn't believe it either, at least the girlfriend part, 'cause that's just crazy. But it's all true."

"I never said anything about a girlfriend."

"Dude, face it, you've got a girlfriend." He poked me in the ribs. "A g-i-r-l-f-r-ahhh . . . end."

I glanced at Dad. I hoped he wasn't listening to this part. "No, Vicki's my friend, and she's a girl, but that's not the same thing."

"I know what I'm talking about," Hardy said. "You have a girlfriend. A g-i-r — "

"I know how to spell it."

"That's 'cause you have one."

I was just about to punch him when Dad finally spoke up. "So that's what's been bothering you. Girlfriends are nice." He nodded and grinned. "No reason to be ashamed about that, even when they almost kill you. That's part of the deal. They're not really your girlfriend until they almost kill you."

"Do you believe me? About the ghosts, I mean?"

"It's crazy like Hardy said, but I don't think you'd make up something like that, even with the chocolate fiend's help, especially not girlfriends. That's going too far." He mussed my hair.

"What about your job? I don't want you to lose it."

Dad put his arm around me and squeezed. "Trey, I know I said I was excited, but that's because I knew I'd be able to do more for you and your mom now. A job is just what I do, it's not who I am. Who I am is a guy who raised a son who's so brave and cares so much about his grandma and his girlfriend that he's willing to stick his head into another dimension to save them. That's worth more than any job in the world." He winked. "I'm really proud of you. Let's go rescue your grandma, and Vicki."

"See?" Hardy said, poking me in the ribs. "Girlfriend."

"Shut up!"

Dad started up the engine. He threw the truck in gear and stomped on the gas. "We can eat rice casserole for a while longer. I'm used to it, and that pizza nearly did me in. Who wants to work for a criminal anyway?"

"Thanks, Dad."

We raced off to Ghostville. Now I just had to figure out what to do when we got there.

CHAPTER EIGHTEEN
PULL THE PLUG

Dad flew through town, honking and weaving in and out of traffic on the way to the Dino Barn/Ghostville. Hardy spilled out a thousand ideas for defeating Rangler.

"We don't have any ray guns." I checked my pockets to make sure. "Or teleporters. And those rocket-powered farts aren't real."

"Dude, you lie. I'm sure about the farts. That egress thing was killer stinky."

"No time machines either," Dad said. "But that is a good idea to go back to fix things before they happen. Then I wouldn't have to miss my lunch break."

Normally I can listen to Hardy's schemes all day long, and still spend the evening cleaning up and explaining why I shouldn't be grounded. But time was running out. We had to free Grandma and Vicki before Rangler got his permanent ghost prison up and running.

"They've been putting in some heavy-duty power lines," Dad said. "And big backup generators. Looks like they want whatever they're powering to survive a nuclear war."

"I saw those yesterday," I said. "Rangler said that once he put the ghosts in the display they can never escape. We have to get there before he turns all that stuff on. When are they supposed to finish with the power lines?"

Dad frowned. "Um, well, I think it was today. The Dino Barn is closed for the work. We better hurry."

My stomach turned. The one at the old museum had kept Wethermerry trapped without the huge power lines. This new one was different. Rangler had said he could control the ghosts at Ghostville, and Wethermerry had still been free to move around inside the museum. Maybe that's what the extra power was for: strings to make the puppets dance. We didn't have much time.

Dad kicked the pedal and I jerked back against the seat. Hardy's candy bar shot out the window as we flew through traffic like a rocket-powered fart.

When we pulled up behind the Dino Barn, Dad let Hardy and me out. I saw Brick's van parked by the loading dock. A brand new transformer hummed and buzzed in the parking lot.

"We're too late."

Dad shook his head. "No way. You two get inside where it's safe. I'll take care of the power. Hopefully the backup isn't running yet."

I stood back and stared at Dad while he pulled a thick cable out of the winch on his truck and wrapped it around the transformer. He connected it back to the other end of the cable and climbed back in. "Good thing they trust me with a big truck. Now get going. Once I've pulled the plug you won't have forever. The backup generators may be close to going online. Oh, and don't touch anything electrical or metal, just in case."

"Just in case of what?" Hardy asked.

"ZZZZZZZZZZZZZZZZ."

"Ouch."

I pulled my ecto-meter out and turned it on. I crossed my fingers, hoping we were close enough for Grandma to get my text.

C-o-m-i-n-g, I typed.

"Trey," Dad said, leaning out the truck window. "I'll follow you in after I pull this thing loose. Don't try to take on Rangler by yourself. He's too dangerous."

I nodded and then Hardy and I made the dash for the loading dock.

"I kind of wanted to stay and see the transformer explode," Hardy said once we'd crept up to the backdoor. "That'd be cool. BOOM! But you'd never get anywhere without my help."

I glared at him. He laughed and punched me, but this time he was right. I was glad to have my best friend helping me again.

Luckily the door was open and no alarms went off. Brick must have forgotten to lock up.

When I'd been inside the Dino Barn the first time I'd noticed that there was a whole other huge section to the building that wasn't being used for the dinosaur exhibits. That had to be where Rangler was setting up the haunted house. Waving Hardy on, I rushed inside. We ran past boxes and crates marked "dino-parts," "ghost-sheets," and "flashing suits." Rangler needed backups for everything.

We were lucky that the museum was closed. The last two days had been a sneak peek. Today there were no crowds, and no one seemed to be on the job either. Maybe Rangler wanted to keep his ghosts a secret until the last moment. Once we reached the exhibit floor we crept behind a Tyrannosaurus robot to scout out the scene.

"Wow, these robots are so cool." Hardy stared up at the mechanical jaws hanging over our heads. "I wonder if you can ride them. That would be awesome."

I shrugged. I didn't have time to think about any new amusement park rides. Although a Tyrannosaurus ride would be cool.

"Try to find that black ball before the power goes out," I said. "Once it's dark, we won't be able to see it and we'll have to act fast before the power comes back on."

"Aren't we waiting for your dad?"

"If there's time."

I crossed my fingers. How long could Vicki survive in that ball? Ghosts could get by without food and water, and a bathroom, but Vicki needed all of those. I wished we'd had more time and a better plan.

"I bet you could crawl up inside that dino and get to the controls," Hardy said. "There's a little hatch right here." He pointed at small door on the dino's belly.

"We don't have time. We need to find that ball."

"I never saw the ball before. What does it look like?"

"Yes you did. That's what they used to suck up Vicki."

"What?"

"It's a small black ball." I held out my hands to bowling ball size. "Black, you know, and a ball. Black ball."

"Gotcha. Black ball. Not too big."

"Don't touch it though. You might end up inside . . . with Vicki."

"No problem there," he said. "So where is it? I don't see anything except dinos."

He was right. We weren't going to find ghosts in the Dino Barn. Looking down at the far end of the hall I spotted a huge arched doorway with another box office next to it. It looked like another entrance, but what hung above made me doubly sure: a brand new *This Way to the Egress* sign.

The fake exit light wasn't lit yet.

"In there." I grabbed Hardy's sleeve. "We've got to get the ghosts out before that sign comes on."

"Why don't we just smash it like the other one?"

"Hey, yeah," I said. "Good idea. Let's bust it up."

Hardy was way ahead of me. Sprinting across the hall straight toward a collection of petrified dino poops, he snatched up a handful and headed for the sign. Based on his aim, I was pretty sure we'd be there all day.

Hardy reared back and chucked his first baseball-sized poop fossil up at the sign. It was a miracle. It crashed right into the big *E*. But there were no flashes or fireworks or rain of glass, just a dull clunk. The rock bounced off, fell back and hit Hardy in the shoulder.

"Ouch! What gives?"

"I don't think it's glass." These lights looked harder than concrete. "Rangler made it unbreakable this time."

"That crud," Hardy said. "Don't worry. Dino poop can do anything."

Gripping his load tightly, he tossed another chunk of poo.

Clunk.

Nothing.

Just then a huge crashing sound came from outside. All the lights flickered and then blinked out. *Dad.*

"Hey, it did work," Hardy said, throwing his last poop anyway. "Just a little slow."

"Way to go, Dad!" I pumped my fist. Then I heard a whoosh and a slam. The doors around the hall clanged shut and locked in one gigantic bang. Cutting the power must have activated some emergency security system leaving Dad stuck outside — and Hardy and me trapped inside. My whole body went cold. We were on our own.

CHAPTER NINETEEN

HALL OF GHOSTS

I tugged at one of the Dino Barn doors. Hardy pulled on another. They stuck fast. Every entrance had smashed closed when Dad destroyed the transformer and cut the power supply, trapping Hardy and me inside and Dad on the outside. I took a deep breath and told myself it would be okay. I could do this, Hardy was with me. But the nagging thought of Vicki turning into a ghost made me shiver.

"Can't wait for my dad," I said, shaking off the creepy feeling in my arms and legs. Then I typed, "I'm coming, Grandma," into my ecto-meter. I waved the meter around to get better reception. There was no answer. I needed to get closer.

Luckily there were no real doors between the dino hall and the ghost room, just some turnstiles. I pushed through the nearest one but forgot to warn Hardy.

WHAM!

"Ouch! That hurts. I need those parts," he whimpered.

Hardy must have been getting used to talking about his feelings.

"Ssssshh!"

Hardy's whining about his broken parts echoed through the hall. What looked like three or four flashlights popped on in the darkness.

"Get down," I said. "They'll see us."

"I can't bend over. I'll never walk again."

Hardy stood his ground, sticking out like a beacon of pain shining on our covert operation. The lights spun around and lit him up like a bull's-eye.

My eyes hadn't adjusted to the dark yet and all I could see were bright spots. I rubbed them, and when I looked back I spotted four men standing around something still too black to make out. One of the men had a giant mustache, another held a ghost vacuum. Rangler and Brick.

"Get them!" Rangler waved his hands and his flashlight beam whipped around the room like a firefly in a tornado. "And see about the power!"

Brick dropped the vacuum and shot off after us along with the other two guards.

I spun around, looking for a place to hide. This time *I* cracked into the turnstile.

I fell into Hardy and tried to grab his arm to keep from going all the way over.

The jolt cured his injury. "I'm outa here!" He raced back into the dino hall. I flopped on the floor like a fish on the beach.

Brick leaped over me and the other two guards followed right behind him, ignoring me.

Rex Rangler aimed his flashlight at my face and reached into his pocket. I waited for him to pull out a stun gun, or maybe to suck me into his ghost prison. But in a second his suit flashed on. Strings of lights lit up the room like a holiday parade. This suit had ghost figures on it.

"That's better." He squinted at me, his gargantuan eyebrow wings flaring. "You again. Who are you, anyway?"

"Trey Newton."

Tilting his head back, Rangler scratched his chin. "Newton, Newton, sounds familiar. Didn't I just hire a Newton? You aren't related, are you?"

"That's my dad, and he just shut off your power." I

wondered if I should be telling him this, but I kind of felt like I was in a movie, taunting my nemesis.

"The payroll needs trimming anyway."

I should have kept my mouth shut.

Rangler wiggled his forehead and his eyebrows danced up and down like hairy worms. "Well now that you've helped me sort out my human resources problem, suppose you tell me why you keep getting in my way."

It was too late to save Dad's job, so I spilled the whole story. "I'm here to rescue my grandma and my friend and put an end to your evil ghostnapping plans."

Rangler's eyes flashed. "There's that awful word again, ghostnapping. If it really is a word, which it's not. Very commendable, however, your devotion to your grandmother. She's not here."

"Yes, she is. I saw her." I stood up and pointed at the black ball lying at Rangler's feet. "She's in there, with all the other ghosts you captured. And she wants out."

Rangler turned sideways and gave the ball a kick. His foot thudded against it and he cried, "Ouch!" It barely skittered across the floor. "Impossible. It's just a ball," he said, rubbing his foot.

"I was in it. I saw everything."

Rangler put his foot down and squinted at me. "So you think that having a haunted house is bad for some reason."

"No, I think kidnapping ghosts is bad."

He walked straight at me, pointing his finger in my face. "Don't you like fun? Ghosts are fun, you know. Scary fun."

"Ghosts are people." I pushed his finger away. "And you can't just put them in prison and use them for a show. That's illegal . . . and wrong."

Laughing, Rangler grabbed my hand and held it. "So you're a lawyer, too? Well, Mr. Lawyer, show me where it's illegal to use ghosts for an amusement park. In fact, show me any law that even mentions ghosts." He dropped my hand and waited for a second, staring at me. "No? I thought not. Ghosts have no rights. They're dead."

"So? They're still people."

"Ridiculous. Ghosts are not people anymore. They're ectoplasmic remnants without any soul. If you watched my TV show, you'd know that."

"I did watch your show," I said. "It *was* my favorite."

"*Was? Was?* Well goody for you. But it *wasn't* enough people's favorite. Cancelled. Gone." He threw his hands in the air and spun around in a circle. "That's why I'm here, rescuing this stupid town. No more TV for Rex Rangler."

"That's no excuse for kidnapping my grandma."

He snapped the light beam in my face. "You aren't listening. *Your grandma is gone! Forever!* Ghosts are like an echo ringing through the canyons. Nobody believes an echo is really a person talking. Ghosts are not people either."

That's exactly what I'd thought before I met Wethermerry and saw Grandma. I'd only wanted to find ghosts so I could become famous. Vicki believed, but I didn't. But now that I had seen Grandma I knew ghosts were people. She was my grandma, not an echo in a canyon. And I loved her.

"That's a lie. I talked to my grandma. She is a person. She's the same as she always was, just a little harder to touch. And she wants out."

"Nonsense," Rangler said. "And that's not going to happen. Those ghosts, or should we call them echo-plasm? Hey, that's clever. *Echo-plasm*. Get it? I combined echo with ectoplasm. Pretty funny, huh?"

"Pretty lame."

"No, it is funny. Hee, hee. Anyway, those echo-plasms are worth millions of dollars to me," Rangler said. "When people discover that I can control real ghosts, they'll come from everywhere to see, and pay to do it. I won't need TV to be famous. And this town will get back on its feet again, people will work. Maybe even your dad will find another job. Who knows? It's possible. Don't you want that? Don't you want to see people happy and working again? Or are the echoes of the dead more important to you than the living?"

I did want my dad to get another job, especially since I'd just lost him his new one. But the ghosts didn't belong to him.

And not all the people in that black hole were ghosts.

"My friend is in there too. And she's still alive. I'm pretty sure that kidnapping girls is illegal."

Rangler froze like a popsicle at the South Pole. "There's that ugly word again. What kidnapping? What girl?"

"Vicki."

"What's a Vicki?"

"She's my friend, the one who asks all the questions," I said.

"Funny, she looked more like a Glissandra to me. Oh, well. So?"

"So Brick sucked her up inside that thing of yours," I said, pointing to the ball. "He put her in there with the ghosts, but she's not a ghost."

"That's a lie, my friend," he said. "Clever, but still a lie. What you're describing is impossible." He turned and walked over to a laptop computer sitting on a table near the ball. "We make videos of every ghost echo we capture, so I'll prove that there's no 'Vicki' inside there."

I watched as the light from the screen danced across Rangler's face. Suddenly he looked around in a panic, his eyes glazing over, searching for something he couldn't see. "You're lying. There's no girl in there. There can't be. You're just trying to make me let the ghosts out. Well, it's not going to work."

"You saw her, didn't you?" I said. "Vicki's inside that thing, and you better let her out."

"No! No! Impossible! Where are those lights?" Rangler yanked at his hair like he was trying to put out a fire. "Why doesn't anyone listen?!"

He looked away and stared at the floor, whispering to himself. "It's not true. It's not true. Everything is going according to plan. You did everything right. Nothing is wrong."

In another second Rangler turned back to me. "Go away, you're bothering me."

"Not without Vicki, and my grandma."

BANG!

We both jerked around at the sound of crashing from the dino hall. Things were falling like dominoes, one after the other. The whole place roared like it was collapsing, dino robots and skeletons smashing to the ground. Then a scream like a wounded donkey echoed through the room. They had Hardy too.

A second later the emergency backup lights snapped on. In the dim light I could see prop fronts of rickety old buildings from old towns that had been torn down. Next to them were decaying graveyards surrounded by iron fences. Stuffed black cats stared down at me from gnarled trees, and fake bats bounced up and down overhead. And in the middle of the room was a black spot, an immense hole to another world. The size of a hot-air balloon, it hovered twenty feet off the floor, steaming and hissing. The permanent containment unit.

"Welcome to Ghostville." Rangler swept his arms out in a spin. He acted like he'd never seen me before. "You're the very first visitor. How do you like it?"

"I want my grandma, and Vicki."

"Stubbornness is sometimes a good characteristic." Rangler dashed back to his laptop. "But not in your case." He punched the keyboard. "Give me a second, and I'll grant your wish."

Beep, beep.

My pocket buzzed. I pulled out my ecto-meter and looked at the green letters scrolling by.

Trey, it's Grandma. Please help. Something's happening.

Green steam erupted in gigantic bursts, fogging over the whole exhibit hall. Rangler typed in more commands.

Beep, beep. Another message scrawled across the screen. *Trey, it's me, Vicki. Why didn't you tell me it was so weird in here?*

I did, I wrote back. *Are you okay? What's going on?*

Vicki typed, *The ghosts are starting to fade, and these stairs that go nowhere are moving, they're collapsing on us. I've got an idea. Why don't you —*

I didn't have time to read, besides, I was pretty sure what she was going to say. Sprinting across the room I raced to get to the computer before Rangler finished. I reached out to knock the computer away, but he threw out a hand and pushed me to the floor like I was nothing. I slid away in a big heap.

Sometimes being a kid sucks.

Rangler punched the last key, roaring with laughter. The balls outside peeled away like smoke in the wind and a stream of wispy forms took shape in the mist. They separated from the black hole and hovered around the room. The pink lady with her yappy poodle twirled and spun around me. Wethermerry stalked by with his musket and coonskin cap while Mr. Greensocks took tickets.

And there was Grandma.

"Grandma! It's me!"

She didn't hear or see me. Her face was blank, her

eyes unblinking. She waltzed right on by like I wasn't there.

"Do you like it?" Rangler laughed. "Isn't it wonderful? So real, so lifelike. Well not lifelike, but afterlifelike. Get it? *Afterlife*like? Ha! I need to write all these great catchphrases down. Pure gold. Anyway, it's a miracle, and it's going to make me famous, *more* famous. I'll never be cancelled again." He reeled and danced right along with the ghosts.

Beep beep. The ecto-meter chirped again.

Help Trey! I feel funny, like I'm fading too. I think I might —

The screen went blank.

Fading? That didn't sound good.

A few seconds later I spotted a short girl with long brown hair emerge from the cloud around the ball, chewing on a huge wad of gum.

It was Vicki.

CHAPTER TWENTY

GRAND OPENING

I stood in the middle of Ghostville, watching the giant containment unit buzz and Rex Rangler cackle with glee. The hall filled with ghosts. Misty, transparent shapes flew everywhere. Rangler must have captured every ghost in the state.

Ghosts wandered through the creaking old houses, popping out from behind doors and flying through windows. They laughed and screamed in my face. My skin crawled, but not because I was scared of the ghosts. I was scared *for* them. They should be free to live their afterlives the way they wanted, not as puppets in an amusement park.

"Vicki?" I looked up and down for her. "Vicki! Answer me!" I crossed my fingers, hoping she wasn't one of the puppets.

A ghost floated by my head, smacked her gum and drifted away to stir a smoking cauldron.

"Vicki!"

She didn't answer or even look, just kept on stirring the pot.

I noticed Rangler poke the screen. The ghosts moved to a new spot and let out howling noises. He *was* pulling their strings.

"Stop it! They're people!"

Rangler laughed and flicked the screen again. Grandma scooped up the ghost of a cat and flew over my head, cackling like a witch. She'd never have dreamed of doing that when she was alive. I was pretty sure she didn't know how to fly, plus she was allergic to cats.

I had to do something. This haunted show could go on forever. People would line up for tickets and walk through the exhibit, pointing and gawking at Grandma for years and she'd never be free. My class would come, just like we did to the opening of the Dino Barn. I could hear them laughing and screaming and making fun of the ghosts. Mr. Brakenbush might wonder what happened to Vicki and how weird it was that a ghost looked just like her, even raising her hand all the time. But he'd never guess it was really her. And if I told the police or anyone, who would believe me?

The containment unit hovered like a dark sun. Lightning bolts shot up from the floor, bright beams of energy holding it in the air. It must have gotten its power from someplace other than the lights. Dad's attack on the transformer hadn't shut it down. But if I could cut off that stream the whole thing might stop working.

The closer I moved to the beams of electricity, the more my skin prickled. My hair stood up straight, my ears buzzed, and I started to shake. It was like that time — okay, *times* — that Hardy dared me to pee on the electric fence around the horse pasture we passed on our way home from school.

Stepping back from the waves of electricity, I looked around for something better than my face to disrupt the flow. I felt a lump in my pocket — dino poop, the real stuff. I still had a couple of rocks, so I whipped one out and hurled it into the stream. As the fossil poop hit the electric bolts a fizzling blue crackle leaped through the air, hitting me right between the eyes.

"OUCH!"

I wanted to touch my nose, but I was afraid it wasn't there, just a smoking hole with my brains peeking out.

That hurt! Way worse than peeing on an electric fence!

"Careful." Rangler wagged his finger. "No touching."

My head twirled as fast as the spirits that spun around the room. Everything I'd tried blew up in my face. The way Rangler laughed I was pretty sure I'd end up another ghost like Vicki.

Vicki.

As fast as I could I texted,

How do I cut backup power?

I stared at the screen but there was no answer. Maybe Vicki wasn't in there anymore. Maybe she really had become a ghost and was floating around the room with the others. A cold stone dropped into my stomach.

The room shook like an earthquake that rattled the floor so hard I almost fell over again. Rangler stopped laughing and turned toward the entrance. His jaw dropped and he grabbed the computer and ducked behind the streams of electricity.

We weren't alone.

Charging through the door and stomping on the turnstiles was a giant tyrannosaurus robot. It smashed into the hall, huge metal mouth hanging open showing foot-long teeth. I gaped at it, my heart racing. I thought dinos were cool, but this one looked like it wanted to eat me.

The dinosaurs were haunted too!

Rumbling like a freight train, the robot took three gigantic steps right at me. I dived out of the way, but the monster followed me toward the far side of the room. Just as I backed into a corner it stopped and the head dropped to the ground, resting its jaw on the floor. Its teeth dripped robot spit. I'd come all this way to rescue ghosts, and now I was going to be eaten by a haunted robot dinosaur.

I gazed at the teeth while I inched further into the corner, my back pressed hard against the wall. There was no more room. I imagined those razor-sharp fangs cutting through me. I opened my mouth to scream when I spotted something behind the teeth.

"Dude, check it out. I'm driving a dinosaur!"

"Hardy?" I let out my breath, really glad I hadn't screamed in front of him.

He grinned and waved. "I jumped in when those

guys chased me. This thing's got controls like a video game. They ran away like chickens. Want to try it? It's awesome."

I had a better idea. "Is there room for me in there, too?"

"No," Hardy said. "It's only got one pilot's seat."

"Rats!" I pointed at the containment unit. "Okay. See if you can stop that electricity."

Hardy's eyes popped. "I thought you said it was a small black ball, that thing's huge."

I shrugged. "I wouldn't need a dinosaur for a small one."

"That's lightning, dude. I could get electrocuted. I remember that electric fence."

I shook my head. "Don't pee on it! Just stick the dino in far enough to cut off the flow."

Hardy shook his head. "I don't know, dude. Lightning."

Maybe he was right. I touched my smoking nose. It was still there, but it hurt like crazy. "I've got a another idea. Can you pick up anything in that mouth?"

Now Hardy's eyes lit up. "I think so. I just have to make sure I don't bite too hard."

I pointed at Rangler, still typing commands into the computer. I didn't care how hard Hardy bit. "Get him!"

Hardy let out a whoop and fired up the robot. It staggered to its feet and turned around. The tail zinged right over my head, parting my hair. Hardy lifted one leg, crashed it down, and then another, stomping right at Rangler. The old TV host cowered behind the protection of the electric arcs. It didn't take Hardy long to forget about getting electrocuted.

"Hardy! Watch out!"

The tyrannosaurus lit up in a spray of blue, green, yellow, and red sparks like a Fourth of July fountain. Electricity streamed over and around its body until it glowed like a rainbow. The legs wobbled and the giant machine leaned over just out of range of the electric arc, ready to fall.

"Hardy!" I screamed, racing over to him. "Hardy? Are you okay?"

"Dude," he whispered, his voice sounding groggy. "Wanna go get a bladder-buster? Buuurrrrpppp!" Then he leaned back, belched again, and rolled up into a ball. I thought I could hear him snoring.

I reached up and pulled on the little door under the T. rex's neck. "Let me in," I said. I yanked on the handle. No luck. The door was stuck fast. "Hardy! Open the door!"

"Later, I'm sleeping."

Hardy was out of it. I needed another answer.

A giant crackle sounded behind me. Vicki's ghost, or whatever it was, hovered nearby, looking at the prison globe. The containment unit sizzled and sparked. Then a small spot the size of Hardy's bladder-buster appeared on the underside. White against the black, it grew bigger and bigger, pushing out like the bump I got on my head when Hardy tested his home-built catapult while I was standing in front of it.

Splurp!

A blob, covered in grayish, dripping, jello-like goo, dropped out onto the floor and rolled out of reach of the electrostatic charges. Then it jumped up into a crouch and raised two hands, fingers extended like talons, up over its head like a ninja.

"EEEEEEYYYYYYAAAAAA!" It screamed and ran straight at Rangler.

Rex glanced over his shoulder at the shout but was too slow to see the goo-blob coming. It took a flying-dragon leap, stuck out its right foot, and kicked Rangler square in the butt like a kangaroo on steroids.

"Hey!" He shrieked and jerked forward, his mustache waving from an impact stronger than a Hardy-powered belch. Stumbling toward the robot, Rangler clanked his head against the dino's left knee and stood there, arching his eyebrows. "Ouch! That hurt!" he cried, rubbing his head.

Then the dino's leg started to creak. First it wiggled. Then it wobbled. Then it waggled. Then it twisted and twined like a rubber band. Finally it buckled. The robot monster tilted and whipped around toward Rangler. I jumped back and the goo-ninja ran the other way. Rangler stood like he was glued in place. The T. rex's mouth gaped open, razor-sharp teeth flashing, and with a roaring crash it smacked down on the hard concrete floor right on top of the ghostnapper. Rows of teeth like prison bars knifed into the floor spreading tiny cracks like spiderwebs around my feet. The teeth surrounded Rangler. He was trapped, eaten by his own fake dinosaur.

A second later the dino's belly popped open. Hardy must have gotten the door unstuck, because he slipped out of the hatch, his hair standing up and his hands shaking. I guessed his nap was over.

"Dude! I think I fried my brains."

"We did it!" I jumped up and down and slapped Hardy on the shoulder.

"Ouch!" He grinned and slapped me back, so I punched him.

He got ready to swing at me when I grabbed his hand. "Come on," I said. "We've got one more thing to do."

I turned around, looking for the goo-thing that had knocked Rangler into his prison. I needed to ask it if Vicki was okay. It was scraping slime from its face.

"Hi, Trey!"

"Vicki!" I cried. "It's you! You're okay!"

"Of course it's me," she said. "Who else do you know who got sucked into a ghost vacuum so you could escape and figure out how to defeat Rangler?" She grinned and wiped more of the sticky gunk away. It covered her entire body with an inch of goo and looked way grosser than the fake dino poop she'd screamed over, but she wasn't acting disgusted now. I must have been getting to her.

"I was scared when you didn't answer my message," I said. "How did you get out?"

"Easy. Everyone else in there was a ghost and couldn't touch anything. Then I remembered how I pulled you out before, so I just decided to push, and boom! I'm here. It was pretty gross though," she added, wiping a handful of goo on me.

"Yuck!" I said. She was learning.

Vicki giggled. "Why's your nose all red?"

"I tried to stick my face in a bolt of lightning."

"Why are you always shoving your head into things?" She reached up and smeared some gunk on my nose. "I think this acts like an insulator. That's why I didn't get electrocuted."

"Hey, that feels good," I said, rubbing the cool slime into my nose. "Thanks."

Just then her ghost zoomed by and floated right in between us. Vicki stopped and her mouth gaped open. "Is that me?" she asked. "I don't chew my gum that way. That's gross." She waved her hand at her apparition. "Go away. Get lost!" Then she kicked at it. The gum-smacking ghost flew up to the ceiling.

"I don't get it," I said. "How can both of you be here at the same time? Aren't those the real ghosts?"

Vicki shook her head. "I don't think so. The ghosts are still trapped. Those are just projections. And not very good ones. My hair does not look like that."

I decided not to tell her that it did.

"Sure it does," Hardy said. "But worse."

Vicki slapped him with a handful of gunk.

"But you said you were fading," I said.

"It felt like that," Vicki said. "I think some sort of projector scanned me and I started to turn invisible. But then I came back. That's when I figured out how to climb out."

"Wait," I said. "If the ghosts aren't out yet, then we still have work to do."

Vicki nodded. "You're right. Let's go!" she said, snapping back into her ninja pose.

Rangler had dropped the laptop when he fell. Vicki and I raced over and she said, "I think you should hit control —"

No time. I jumped up and down on it, smashing the machine into tiny pieces. I'd always wanted to do that. "Now we're done," I said.

Nothing happened.

I looked over at the giant floating black hole and stopped cold. The containment ball still hummed and the ghosts still danced.

Rangler laughed from behind his tooth prison. "Problem?"

I shivered. "I broke the computer," I said to Vicki. "Why aren't the ghosts free?"

"Um," Vicki said. "I was going to say that if you hit control-F10-delete, I think that's how you deactivate it."

"How did you figure that out?"

"A ghost told me," she said.

"Okay." I leaned over and punched the keys. Little plastic lettered squares fell out on the floor, cracked and broken. "Rats!"

"Now what do we do?" Vicki asked.

There was only one thing left. I leaned into the teeth and grabbed Rangler's coat. "How do we shut the containment unit down and let the ghosts free?"

When I grabbed him, Rangler's mustache slipped off his lip and dangled around his neck. It was fake too. The only things that were real were the ghosts, and possibly his eyebrows.

"Sorry to disappoint you," he said, brushing my hands away and straightening his jacket. "But I'll just wait for the police to come and arrest you. I'm sure they'll take my side. I'm a big man in this town. I'm famous."

I looked at Vicki and Hardy. "We have to turn that thing off."

Hardy shook his head and threw up his hands. "The dino didn't work. And I busted up that egress sign pretty good."

Rangler laughed again and his suit flashed in a rainbow of colors. "I'm the only one who knows how to turn it off, and I'm not telling."

This guy was seriously crazy. I had no more ideas, and another dinosaur wasn't going to come crashing through the door.

Just then my ecto-meter beeped. The screen read: *suit.*

"Suit? What does that mean?"

Rangler snorted. "You'll never get it. Probably means *lawsuit*, which is coming your way. I hope your parents have money. Oh, that's right, someone's dad just lost his job." He snickered again, turned a knob on his remote control, and the rainbow switched to flashing red like a stop light.

I texted back.

I don't get it.

I stared at the screen, waiting for an answer. Nothing.

"What's the answer?" I shouted at the ball.

Still no text.

I slapped at my head and looked at Hardy, but he just shrugged. "Beats me."

The ecto-meter beeped. *Suit*, was all it said.

An idea struggled to get out of my head. I'd noticed Rangler tuck the control back in his pocket. Is that what the message meant, his clothes? I only had one choice. I shoved my head in again. Then I reached through the tyrannosaurs's teeth and yanked the controls for Rangler's Christmas tree suit out of his pocket.

"No!!!! Give that back!"

Jackpot!

I put my thumb on the switch.

Rangler screamed, wild-eyed. "Don't! It's booby-trapped. You'll blow up the whole town!"

I looked at Vicki. "He's lying," she said, shaking her head. "I hope."

She didn't sound too certain.

"No way," Hardy said. "But that would be cool."

I squeezed the control box.

"Listen, kid," Rangler said, holding his hands together and pleading. "I'll give your dad his job back. Even let your grandmother go. Just don't push that button. You'll ruin me. You don't want that. Remember all the fun times you had watching my shows? I was your favorite."

I looked at Vicki and grinned. "You *were* my favorite." Then I flipped the OFF switch. Suddenly the sizzling electricity under the ball exploded, shooting up to the ceiling in huge zigzags of lightning. The whole building rocked with thunder.

Vicki, Hardy, and I ran for cover.

I blew up the whole town!

Then the crackling stopped, and the lightning bolts shrank back into the floor. The containment unit still hung in the air, but after a few seconds it started to shimmer and flash just like Rangler's clothes. In a rush the ghosts stopped screeching and swooping and winked out.

"Where'd they go?" Hardy asked. "You killed them."

Uh-oh.

"No, look." Vicki pointed at the ghost ball.

The outside of the giant sphere slowly peeled away as wispy layers wafted into a thin mist. Then with a great *SPLAT*, like a Hardy-tossed water balloon hitting me in the face, a downpour of goo splashed onto the floor. Fog steamed up from the giant puddle. From the cloud, one by one, shadowy figures emerged and floated out to encircle us, laughing and hugging each other. The ghostly howls were replaced by the roar of cheering and hands clapping.

"We're free! We're free! You did it! We're free!"

Grandma glided up and wrapped her arms around me, although she still couldn't touch me. "Oh, Trey. I knew I could count on you. You're such a smart, grown-up, brave boy."

I tried to hug her back, but ended up hugging myself.

"Thanks Grandma. I'm glad you're okay."

She smiled big and wide, beaming at me. I could feel her glow all through my body. We were going to be together again.

I felt warm all over. "Vicki, did you meet my Grand —?" I looked around for Vicki. She wasn't there.

Grandma hovered beside me. "Don't worry, dear, she'll be here in a second. She's a little busy right now."

I glanced around the room, finally spotting Vicki by the old movie theater set. A man in an Army uniform knelt on one knee in front of her. She nodded and waving her arms threw a kick. She must have been telling her story.

"You have a very nice girlfriend," Grandma said.

Hardy snickered. "See, g-i-r-l-f-ahhh, whatever. I told you."

"Shut up!"

I looked at Grandma. "Who is that she's talking to? Is that her — "

She nodded. "Yes."

In another minute Vicki and the ghost soldier walked over to Grandma and me.

"Trey," Vicki said, beaming. "This is the man who figured out how to turn off the controls and taught me that flying kick. Meet my dad."

CHAPTER TWENTY-ONE

MOVING ON

Vicki and I sat on the floor in the middle of Ghostville with my Grandma and her dad. The ghosts were all free now, and Rangler was down for the count.

"This is so great that we can all be here," Vicki said, smiling wider than I'd ever seen. Her face was easier to see now that she'd washed most of the goo off. "I always wanted you to meet my dad."

Her dad, whose name was Jacob Winters, Sergeant Jacob Winters, knew all about electronics and had figured out Rangler's secret controls. "I'm glad to see Vicki is making new friends," he said. "You both should be proud of yourselves."

Vicki touched my hand. "Good job. I knew I could count on you."

"You too," I told her.

She looked over at Rangler, trapped in his dino prison. He sat on the floor, twirling his moustache. "You got him." She smiled.

"*We* got him."

My heart beat like a hummingbird's wings, what with her dad right there, but I grabbed Vicki's hand and helped her up. Hardy giggled.

"Shut up!"

"Told you," he said.

Vicki looked down at her hand in mine and then over at her dad, who smiled at her. "I always feel safe when my dad holds my hand. He's the best." Then in a whisper so her dad couldn't hear, "He likes you. He thinks you're really brave."

Hardy heard. He gagged on his finger.

Vicki slapped his shoulder. "Grow up!"

★ ★ ★

Well, now that I'd found real ghosts, set them free, become friends with the weird girl, lost my dad his job, and defeated evil for all time, I sat down to talk to Grandma. I had my plans all ready for her to move in with us. She could have my bedroom and I'd get the one downstairs. Then I wouldn't have to listen to my dad snoring and Hardy and I, and Vicki too, could play video games without being nagged. And since Grandma was a ghost she didn't need to eat. Maybe she could even help Dad get another job by scaring somebody into hiring him. It was a perfect plan without any holes.

"What do you think, Grandma? I haven't told Mom or Dad yet, but Dad is outside and knows all about you and the other ghosts. I'm sure it won't be a problem. He even helped me by shutting down the power." I nodded in agreement for her. "It'll be great. Maybe you could even help me find other ghosts and get on TV. I know you probably don't want to be famous, but maybe someone else does."

Grandma smiled and stroked my hair, or pretended to. "You mean like you?"

"I'm pretty much over that." I glanced at Rangler, stuck in his dino-tooth cell. "Famous isn't so great."

"Oh, Trey, you're such a sweet, sweet boy," she said. "I love you so much. Nothing would make me happier than to come and live with you and have you sit on my lap again while I read you stories."

I knew I was too big for her lap, but the rest sounded good.

"I'll tell Dad," I said, jumping up.

Grandma grabbed at my hand. "But . . ."

I stopped and looked back at her. "But what?"

"But I'm afraid it doesn't work that way."

"What do you mean? What doesn't work that way?"

Grandma smiled and looked around, motioning toward the other ghosts. I hadn't noticed before, but they were all gathered together in a group at the far end of the hall. A few stopped to shake their fists at Rangler, who was still trapped inside the tyrannosaurus's mouth, but then they quickly joined the others. One by one all the ghosts started to shimmer and flicker, like a lightbulb about to burn out. In a few seconds they were gone.

"What's happening? Are they going back to haunt their old houses? I think most of them were torn down. We might have to find other places for them to haunt. Maybe the old museum?"

"No, dear." Grandma's voice was soft, sounding like when she'd first told me that she was sick. "It's time for them to go. They're moving on. Most ghosts only stay a while, but we were trapped here by that awful man until you rescued us. Our time here is over. My time is over."

I choked on my breath and the room shrank in around me. "No. You can't go, not now that I set you free."

"But you did set me free," Grandma said. "It's time for me to use that freedom."

"What about Vicki's dad?" I turned toward Vicki. She and her dad were back by the old movie theater that she'd told me they'd always gone to. She wasn't practicing kicks anymore. This time she was wiping her eyes.

"We all have to go." Grandma smiled big and bright and a glow emerged from behind her eyes, streaming out to touch me with its warmth. The shine quickly spread to her whole body and she turned so bright I had to squint to see her. In another second she drifted toward the ceiling and flickered like the others.

"Bye, Trey," Grandma said with a little wave of her hand. "I love you. You'll always be my hero."

I watched her float off and slowly fade away. This time I was there to see her leave.

"Bye, Grandma." I didn't care if Hardy saw me cry. "I love you, too."

And then she was gone. Forever.

I sniffed and wiped my eyes. Vicki walked over. She

hung her head and looked down at her feet, her face hidden behind her bangs. She held out her hand and I took it.

Her dad had faded away, too. All the ghosts had left. All except one.

* * *

Vicki, Hardy and I stood in the hallway after school, waiting for all the other kids to clear out. Vicki double checked for teachers and then popped a wad of gum into her mouth. She chomped excitedly as I prepared to get a failed bubble spit at me. I'd tried to show Vicki how to blow bubbles, but I'm not any good either and we both got tired of picking gum out of each other's hair.

"Okay." She scanned her checklist. "Tomorrow's Saturday so we have to get up early to go to the cemetery to mow and weed around Wethermerry's statue."

Hardy groaned.

"I already have to mow my own lawn," I said. "My dad's teaching me to cut straight lines."

"Trey." Vicki put her hands on her hips. "You promised. We told Wethermerry that in exchange for helping us find lost ghosts, who we could help move on, we'd keep his gravesite clean. Besides, I asked your dad and he said you could wait until Sunday to do your yard work."

That's what I get for inviting Vicki over for pizza. She conspires with Dad.

"And look." She waved a sheet of paper at me. "I've got the petition to make the second Saturday in August Wethermerry Lewis Founder's Day, with a parade, fireworks, ice cream, and everything. After we mow and scrub the statue we have to go out and get signatures."

Signatures?! Mowing?! Scrubbing?! How come nobody told me being friends with a girl was so much work? Well, nobody but Hardy, but who listens to him?

"But that statue is covered with bird poop. It's yucky."

Vicki shook her head. "You promised."

Suddenly I got goose bumps and the feeling I was being watched. Vicki smiled at something behind me, and even though they'd stopped hating each other I knew it couldn't be Hardy.

"Much obliged to you kids for keeping the old statue pigeon free." Wethermerry floated near the ceiling in his fringed leather jacket and furry hat. He'd decided not to move on until he'd help all the other lost ghosts in town to make up for letting his friends get kidnapped by Rangler. "I'm popular with the birdies," he said, "so the poop's kind of built up over time. It may take a bit of elbow grease — and a strong stomach."

"Bleh!"

Suddenly lawn mowing seemed like fun.

"Pssst." Vicki held back a giggle and put her hand to her mouth so Hardy couldn't hear her. "That's what Hardy's for."

Hardy did have the strongest stomach I'd ever seen, and nobody is more amazed by old poop.

I winked at her and pulled out my ecto-meter. Down to business. I pointed it at the door in front of us. *GIRLS*. I crossed my fingers and hoped Glissandra wasn't in there again. The ecto-meter beeped a couple of times and the little green line on the screen danced up and down.

"Contact. Someone's definitely at home."

"Everybody ready?" Vicki asked.

I nodded and Wethermerry tipped his cap.

"Ready for what?" Hardy said.

"Good. Let's do it. EEEEEEYYYYYAAAA!!!" Vicki screeched, jumped into her ninja stance, arms raised, hands looking like hawk talons, picked up her foot with a high-flying karate kick and planted it right in the middle of the door. It whipped open and we rushed inside. Screams and flying hair filled the air.

Well, at least no one can blame this one on me.

They can't say Vicki isn't supposed to be in the girls' room.

ABOUT THE AUTHOR

John Bladek grew up in Washington — the state, not that other place with all the white buildings. When he was young he liked to listen to ghost stories on the radio and sneak into the basement on Friday nights to watch a scary TV show his mom didn't approve of. He no longer hides under his pillow after visiting the haunted house down the road, but he still remembers those scary tales. Since then John earned a PhD in History, where all ghosts come from, loves to play trivia, and wonders why they don't make hauntable houses anymore.

ABOUT THE
COVER ILLUSTRATOR

Born in the UK in 1988, **Charlie Bowater** was raised on '90s cartoons and as much Disney as she could get her hands on. Growing up, she insisted that one day she would be an animator. Although that changed a little, her love of art never has!

She lives in the North East of England and works as a Senior Concept Artist. The rest of the time she's an illustrator and doodler of anything and everything else.

ACKNOWLEDGEMENTS

Thanks for reading! This is the best part yet.

I know most of you out there, sitting in your rocket ship of a classroom, rollercoaster of a library, or at home where your tablet time has been used up for the day, are thinking that authors are geniuses. We work alone in our magnificent brilliance with two cats and dog in a state you don't live in.

For the most part this is true, except for most of it.

Magnificently brilliant authors? Hmm . . . Let's say . . . oh . . . why not? Yes.

Dogs and cats? If we're lucky.

But authors definitely do not work alone.

"But wait," Anonymous[1] writes, "I've got this essay on Abraham Lincoln's beard and my teacher Ms. Sprinkleton won't let me work with anyone else. I have to write it alone. Not even the internet can help. Am I being discriminated against?"

Sorry to hear that, Anonymous (thanks for writing, by the way). In answer to your question, no, it's not discrimination. Sometimes teachers like their students to learn on their own, to prove themselves, as it were. Or, perhaps Ms. Sprinkleton is hinting for a nice shiny apple on her desk. Either way, good luck with the presidential beard. But you are correct in thinking that in the real world writers don't have to labor alone. We get tons of help. All the time. Every day. Sometimes even from the internet.

Writers get help coming up with good ideas. We get help throwing out bad ideas. Other writers read our work and tell us what they think is awesome and what could be more awesome. Agents read our manuscripts and give more advice, and then they get on the phone and sell our work (yay!) to editors at publishing houses for money, which we use to buy our own islands, and someday soon, our own planets. Then those editors hand out even more advice, like, "Really? Are you kidding? Ghosts *and* dinosaur robots? Who would read that?"[2] After that even more editors make sure all the words in the book are spelled correctly because many people (yes, editors are people) hate misspelled words. From there artists and designers create artsy covers and arrange everything inside the book to look terrific.

At this point something magical has happened. Those words on the screen are now a *real book*. And it did not happen through the work of one brilliant person sitting alone staring at a computer until a story appeared.

So now, I will tell you many, if not all, of the people I am thanking (or acknowledging)[3] for helping me with *Lost in Ghostville*.

First, I'd like to thank the person who helps me the most. Davonna Juroe[4], my friend and a great writer herself, is there for me with all the writing I do. She was with me in my back yard, with *her* dog,[5] where she helped me come up with the idea for *Lost in Ghostville*. Without her, there would be no ghosts in *Ghostville*[6] and Trey may well have been named Monkey Breath.

Second, thanks to all my critique partners. In no particular order, Brad Thiessen, Jessica Young, Joan Magnelli, Dianna Winget, Brandy Dougherty, Bernadette Martonik, Cory Ray, and Deby Fredericks. They're all writers too, good ones, and they read and listened and never said, "Give it up, you ain't got it." Exactly the opposite. Sometimes they even laughed, in a good way. And Trent Reedy, another fine author, who has always been encouraging.

Also thanks to Jamie Weiss Chilton, my agent, who not only encouraged me to add more (shock!) *emotion*, but also got an editor to buy *Ghostville* even after many others gave up their shot at glory.

Thanks to Donald Lemke, the aforementioned[7] editor, who never actually said, "Are you kidding?" but did have good suggestions anyway. And thanks to all the fine people at Capstone, who worked hard to check the spelling in this book, put a cover on it, and made sure the pages didn't fall out when you read it.

Thanks to my local SCBWI group in Spokane, who always put out the effort to support and encourage local writers for young people.

Thanks everyone!

John Bladek

---

[1] Funny name, but if Ms. Sprinkleton doesn't mind, I don't either.

[2] Answer: You.

[3] Vocabulary word. You're welcome.

[4] Isn't that a cool name?

[5] Coda, the best German Shepherd, nee dog, ever, who I call Moose or Bear, 'cause I'm inventive.

[6] I know, crazy. But the dino poop is all mine. I'm not giving that one up.

[7] Another vocabulary word.